Advance Praise for
Orion O'Brien and the Ghost of Samuel Grayhawk

[A]n entertaining tale that will engage young readers while putting history in a context they can understand. Educators should place this book in their recommended reading lists.

NANCY WALLERSTEIN
Former Chair of the Shawnee Indian Mission Foundation

Fran Borin's book, Orion O'Brien and the Ghost of Samuel Grayhawk *is an engaging and modern day ghost story for kids. This is a fun chapter read on its own or could easily be incorporated by teachers as part of a social studies history unit for grades 3rd – 5th.*

RACHEL HOHENDORF
Elementary Teacher, Kansas City, Kansas

I would tell my friends to read this book because it takes place in Kansas and teaches kids something about the history of Native Americans who have always lived in Kansas.

CAITLIN DAILEY
age 9 ½, Fairway, KS

The realistic and gentle dialogue between the main characters provides a great example of children learning to appreciate and respect differences in life experiences and cultural backgrounds. Then the overall focus on relationships delivers a wonderful message outlining how very alike we all are in our basic need for love, family, and friendships.

MELINDA LANG
Library Assistant, Perry, KS

This is a well-researched and heartfelt book that will teach kids (and adults!) about friendship and appreciating each others' differences in a fun, entertaining way. The story has humor, suspense, and strong themes of family and of wanting to find our way home.

Is it possible to discover life and love in a graveyard? …Orion O'Brien and the Ghost of Samuel Grayhawk guides readers on an exploration in a story [showing] the goodness of friendship.

I really liked the book! It was really great to read with references that I recognized. I would like to know if there will be a sequel? Will Orion meet any other ghosts?

MISSION POINT PRESS

Published by Mission Point Press
2554 Chandler Rd.
Traverse City, MI 49696
(231) 421-9513
www.MissionPointPress.com

ISBN: 978-1-958363-14-0
Library of Congress Control Number: 2022907421

Printed in the United States of America

ORION O'BRIEN
AND THE GHOST
OF SAMUEL GRAYHAWK

FRAN BORIN

MISSION POINT PRESS

For Brendan, Colin and Alison

Prologue

Shawnee Indian Mission, Indian Territory: 1845

Samuel and his cousin Thomas sanded the wooden panels on the sides of the cabinet. Their hands were covered in sawdust and their fingers were cramped from pressing the sanding blocks, but the wood needed to be as smooth as a round stone from the stream before it could be waxed. Samuel loved working with wood and was proud of his skill with it, but today he couldn't keep his mind on his work. He kept stopping to stare off in the distance.

"What's wrong with you?" asked Thomas. He spoke in their native language, under his breath. "Don't you want to finish this piece?"

Samuel looked up to see if the master of the woodshop, Mr. Logan, was nearby.

"I have to see Molly," he said quietly. "The matron told me after breakfast that she is very near death. I can't bear to think of losing her!"

Thomas caught his breath. "No! I did not realize she was so sick," he replied. "Surely she can be healed? She is your only sister…what will you do?"

"Boys!"

A voice from behind them startled them both. They whirled around to see Mr. Logan towering over them with a frown on his face.

"Did I hear you speaking a forbidden language?" said Mr. Logan. He had a wooden stick in one hand that he thumped into his palm with a whack. "I won't have any of that 'Injun' talk in my shop! You will speak English only! How else can we make you little savages into respectable people? If I hear more of this today, you'll both be punished." He whacked the stick in his palm again.

"But, Mr. Logan," said Samuel, changing to English now, "my sister Molly is dying, and I must see her before it is too late! She is all that I have left now!"

"That's not possible," said Mr. Logan. "If you visit the sick cabin, you will surely also catch the typhoid fever. I'd hate to lose a promising craftsman like you. Back to your work, now." Mr. Logan walked away to check on another crew of young workers.

"What are you going to do?" asked Thomas as soon as Mr. Logan was out of earshot.

"Look," said Samuel, pointing, "there's a horse by the woodshop door." He carefully laid his sanding block on top of the cabinet. "If Mr. Logan asks where I am, say I went to the well to draw more water."

"Be careful, Samuel!" whispered Thomas. "We don't need more trouble!"

"I know," said Samuel, "but I have to see Molly. She's my only sister."

While Mr. Logan's back was turned, Samuel quickly slipped out the front door of the woodshop and sized up the saddled mare that was tethered to the post. He untied her quietly and spoke soothingly as he guided her away from the woodshop. The stirrup was high for him, but he was wiry and strong and heaved himself onto her back with no trouble. Leaning over her neck, he gripped her mane and clicked his tongue. By the time Mr. Logan came shouting out the woodshop door, all he saw was the dust settling from the mare's hoofbeats.

Fairway, Kansas:
Present Day

Chapter 1
New Neighbors

Do you believe in ghosts? I never did. I mean, maybe in old, musty places with castles and dungeons somewhere, but not in the twenty-first century, and not here in my neighborhood! But that all changed in fifth grade. I saw a real ghost with my own eyes, and I'm a true believer now. If it happened to me—Orion O'Brien, a regular girl living with my mom, dad, my brother Ollie and our dog Butterscotch on a regular block in Fairway, Kansas, U.S.A.—it could happen to *you*.

You might be thinking I believe in the Tooth Fairy and the Easter Bunny, too, but no way. I'm ten, after all. And this didn't happen just to me. Ollie, the two neighbor kids, and even Butterscotch were in on it too. It all started when the Martellis moved in across the street.

I WAS BORED WITH summer, and ready to kill my little brother. So one day in late July when a moving truck parked across the street, I staked out a place at the front window to see if the new people had any kids. Maybe they'd have a girl my age…or maybe a boy! (Ideally a boy a bit older—I didn't tell my mom I was thinking that, lol.) I was pretty disappointed when I saw two kids get out of an SUV—a boy and a girl who were both *little*.

"Geez, the new family just has little kids—nobody old enough for me to hang out with," I complained to my mom.

"Well, maybe you can line up some babysitting jobs in a few months," said Mom. I hadn't thought of that. Mom and Dad had told me I could start babysitting when I turned eleven, which would be in February. "Their mom and dad are busy with moving in, so why don't you go ask if you can help with the kids? We can make some cookies to take over." So she helped us make chocolate chip cookies, and even though Ollie ate half the dough, I had enough cookies to take to the new family that afternoon. Mom made me take Ollie with me.

"Don't say anything stupid," I warned him as we crossed the street. We rang the bell, and while we waited on the porch for someone to open the door, I felt a fuzzy nose on the back of my leg. I turned around and saw Butterscotch wagging her tail on the step with us.

"Ollie!" I cried. "Butterscotch almost made me drop

the cookies! You were supposed to make sure she stayed inside! What if the new people don't like dogs?"

"What?! You never told me to leave her at home," he answered back. "She must have just followed us out the door."

"You better take her back—" Just then the door was opened by a thin boy with dark hair and dark eyes. He was a bit taller than Ollie, but way shorter than me. I had to admit, up close, he looked a little older than I had thought—maybe a fourth-grader. The little girl came up behind him. She also had dark hair, but gray eyes, and looked about five years old. The boy didn't say anything, but the girl looked at Butterscotch and cried, "Ooh, it's a puppy!"

"Hi," I said. "I'm Orion O'Brien, and this is my brother Ollie, and we live across the street in the white house with the red door."

"And this is Butterscotch," said Ollie.

Just then a woman came to the door and joined the kids. "Hello," she said. "I'm Angie Martelli, and this is Salvatore and Sofia. They were hoping there would be some kids on the block. Would you like to come in?"

"Um, do you mind if our dog comes in?" I asked, looking down at Butterscotch. "Ollie was supposed to make sure she didn't follow us, but here she is." Ollie huffed and crossed his arms, but didn't say anything.

Mrs. Martelli invited us all inside. The little girl knelt

down beside Butterscotch and started petting and hugging her.

"We brought you some cookies!" said Ollie, and I handed her the plate.

"How nice!" said Mrs. Martelli. "We just got here from New Jersey last night, so we haven't had time to make treats. We can have them for dessert tonight."

"Dessert?! I want some now!" complained Salvatore.

"Mind your manners," said Mrs. Martelli. She gave us each one cookie.

"I know you're busy with the movers," I said, "so I thought if you need help with the kids, I could take care of them and show them around. I'm ten, and I've lived on this street my whole life."

"Oh, really?" Mrs. Martelli smiled. "Why don't you go to the family room and get acquainted?"

As soon as we got there, Salvatore glared at me. "Don't call me 'Salvatore,' I just go by 'Sal.' And my sister goes by 'Sofi.' And I don't need anyone to 'take care' of me! I'm ten, too."

My jaw almost dropped. "You're *ten*? I had you figured for a third- or fourth-grader," I said.

"Yeah, well, give me time, and I'll be taller than you some day!" he replied. "I had my birthday last month, and I'll be in fifth grade."

"O-kaaay," I said. I wasn't trying to be rude, really! He was so short, what was I supposed to think?

Sofi hardly looked big enough to be in school. "So how old are you?" I asked.

"I'm seven," said Sofi. Her new front teeth had just started growing in.

Ollie and Sofi sat down on the family room floor with Butterscotch, who licked the crumbs off of Sofi's hand. Butterscotch is about a foot high and has curly yellow-brown fur. She loves people, and you could tell she was happy to have somebody new to play with.

"What kind of dog is she?" asked Sofi.

"We don't know for sure," said Ollie. "We adopted her from a shelter when she was a puppy. My dad says she must be part poodle."

Butterscotch was wagging her tail so hard from all the attention, her rear end whipped from side to side. We all laughed.

Sal and Sofi wanted to show us their rooms, so we followed them upstairs. Sal had posters of superheroes and the New York Mets on the wall. He had superhero sheets on his bed, too. Ollie's been asking for those for a year. He flopped down on Sal's bed and hugged the pillow. In Sofi's room, the bed was half covered with stuffed animals, and she had a big toybox and a bookcase. She and Ollie started pulling out toys and books and scattering them all over.

"Let's go to the basement," said Sal. "My dad's going to fix up a playroom for us down there. We'll get new carpet and have our own TV and maybe our own computer." Sal and I took Butterscotch and went downstairs. There was a big, open room that had shelves on one side, and there were a couple of beanbag chairs stashed in one corner.

"We didn't have a playroom in our old house," he said. "There'll be a place for Sofi to do gymnastics, and Mom says we can paint murals on the walls. I'm going to paint the logo for the Mets!"

"Hmmm, I'm a Royals fan," I said.

There wasn't much to see yet—just a big empty room with the washer and dryer at one end, but there was a doorway beside the water heater. "What's back here?" I asked as Butterscotch came up behind me. I opened the door and saw a small room with old wooden shelves all along the back wall. There wasn't even a lightbulb in it, just a little window, and it was pretty dark.

"Just a place to put stuff we're not using," said Sal. Just then Butterscotch started to growl.

"What's wrong, girl?" I asked, and knelt down beside her. "There's nothing to be afraid of." Butterscotch growled some more and suddenly gave a sharp bark. I could feel her quivering as I put my arms around her to try and calm her down. "Quiet, Butterscotch," I said. Sal came and peeked into the little room. There wasn't much there. The shelves were mostly empty, except for some piles of old rags on the bottom shelf.

"This is weird," I said. "She hardly ever barks at anything, and she's usually real quiet. I wonder if there's a mouse down here or something."

"My mom will freak if there is," said Sal. "Let's see if she finds anything."

I let go of Butterscotch, and she bounced over to the shelf at the back of the room. She nosed around at the bottom near the corner, then came back to me. She looked up at me, whimpering and squealing.

"If there was a mouse there, it's gone by now," I said.

"Don't say anything to my mom, OK?" said Sal. "Let's go back upstairs."

Chapter 2

The Indian Mission

We went back up to get Ollie and Sofi, and helped put the toys and books away. Then we all went outside.

"What are those big buildings a couple of blocks over?" asked Sal. "We drove by there yesterday afternoon. Does anybody live there?"

Ollie and I laughed. "You mean the great big brick ones? That's the Shawnee Indian Mission," I said. "You want to go see? Come on!"

Everyone in Fairway knows about the Mission. The buildings are on a giant grassy field that takes up a whole block of the neighborhood. I explained as we walked the couple of blocks to the grounds.

"Years and years ago, it was where Indian—that is, Native American—kids came to go to school," I said. "It closed a long time ago, but kids from lots of different Indian tribes came here. That building over there had schoolrooms, and they slept and ate over there." I pointed to the different buildings.

"We go on a field trip from school almost every year," said Ollie. "And they have a cool festival with Indian dancing and stuff."

"Yeah, that's in the fall," I said, "so you can go to it this year. It's pretty fun. There's people wearing pioneer clothes, and you can go inside and see what the school-rooms looked like." We walked all around one of the buildings. Sal pointed to another brick building at the edge of the grounds.

"Is that part of the Mission too?" he asked.

"Nope, that's a high school," I said. "All these houses and the high school weren't even here back then."

"Some people say the ghosts of the Indian kids are still around here," said Ollie.

"Oh, yeah?" asked Sal. "Has anybody ever really seen one?"

"Are you kidding?" I answered. "It's just silly stories about weird things that happened in their houses, like books falling off a shelf or something. My mom says it's all a bunch of nonsense. But the Mission is pretty cool. Are you going to go to Konza School? You'll for sure go on a field trip to see it."

Sal looked serious. "We went to Catholic school in New Jersey, but I don't know where we're going now." Sal would be in the same grade as me, and Sofi was going into second, a year behind Ollie.

"I hope you'll go to Konza School with us," I said. "It's a great place."

"So, what's 'Konza,' anyway?'" asked Sal.

"It's the Kansas prairie," I said. "It's kind of like 'Kanza,' the Indian tribe that Kansas is named for. 'Kanza' means 'people of the south wind.'"

Sofi and Ollie were under a big tree, and as I watched, Sofi did a standing backflip.

"Wow!" I said, and ran over to her. "That was really good! How did you learn to do that?" Sofi just smiled and shrugged. Ollie's eyes were popping out.

"She started gymnastics when she was four," said Sal. We started to walk back toward home.

"So, what's with your name?" asked Sal. "It's kinda weird. Isn't Orion a star or something?"

"It's a constellation," I explained. "You know, stars that make a shape in the sky. Orion's the hunter. I'll show you when it gets dark. And anyway, I've never known anyone named Salvatore, either."

"It's Italian," said Sal. "My grandparents came from Italy and they can speak Italian, but I only know a few words."

"Bad ones?" asked Ollie.

Sal was grinning. "Yeah, a few," he said.

"Tell me!" said Ollie. Sal laughed and shook his head,

and I rolled my eyes. Like Ollie would have the nerve to say any bad words.

"So," said Sal, "what are you guys? I mean, I'm pretty sure you aren't Italian, but I'm not sure what…. You don't even look like brother and sister."

It's true that Ollie and I don't look much alike—my hair's long, curly, and honey-brown and I have green eyes. Ollie has straight black hair and dark brown eyes. We both have the same suntan-colored skin, though.

"Our dad says we're Heinz 57," said Ollie. "That means a whole lot of things mixed together!"

"Ollie, shut up!" But I grinned at Sal. "That's sort of right, though. Our grandparents are Eastern European and African American and Indian and Irish, which is why our last name's O'Brien!"

"Indian? Like Sitting Bull?" asked Sal.

"Who's Sitting Bull?" asked Sofi.

"No, Sitting Bull was Native American, like the kids at the Mission," I said. "Our dad's mom is from India. We both look *kinda* like our grandparents, just not the same ones!"

As we walked back to our street, Sal told me his dad had gotten laid off from his job in New Jersey, but found a new job here in Kansas. He said that they hadn't had much money for a while, so their family went through a lot of changes.

"My mom's a nurse, and she's looking for a job for

when school starts. I'll have to get Sofi home from school if Mom can't pick us up," he said.

"That'll be easy," I said. "Ollie and I walk to and from school every day. You can always hang out with us, even if you go to Catholic school, or with Betty and Wally next door—they're real nice, and Betty makes lots of cookies and goodies."

Sal sighed. "I wish Mom and Dad would decide soon where we're going to school—I don't like not knowing. And I've never gone to public school before, and it was bad enough that I had to leave all my friends…"

"That must be tough," I said. "I've never had to do that. But if you go to Konza, you'll make lots of new friends there."

By then we were back at our street. Sal and Sofi came to our house for a minute to meet Mom, then went back home. After they left I told my mom how Butterscotch had acted in the Martellis' basement.

"She might have smelled a dog that lived there before, or some other animal," said Mom. "You know dogs can scent something even after it's gone away."

"I don't know," I said. "She seemed really freaked about something."

"Well, there's always a logical explanation, even if we don't know what it is right away," said my mom. That's what she always says, and I had always believed her when she said it.

Chapter 3

Freaky Lights

As it turned out, it was great having the Martellis right across the street. We could hang out together at our house even if Mom was busy. She's an accountant, and works from her office at home. My two best friends, Mady and Taylor, were both out of town on vacation and wouldn't be back until right before school started. It was pretty cool to have someone my own age to talk to, even if it was a boy.

A couple of days after they moved in, Ollie and I were at the Martellis' (without Butterscotch), and Sal asked me to help him take some things to the basement. He was still putting his room together and decided he'd outgrown some of his toys and books. We both took an armful of stuff and Sal led the way down the steps and switched on the light. We stacked the things on a bookcase in the playroom, and I turned around to follow Sal back upstairs. That's when I saw a shadow move through the little room behind the water heater, where sunlight came in from the window above. "Is somebody down here?" I called.

"Mom's upstairs and Dad's at work," Sal said. "I didn't see anything." He was right, there couldn't be anybody there, but just to make sure, I stepped toward the little room and stuck my head inside the door. Just then, the light flickered off and on a few times. I whipped back around and looked at Sal in surprise.

"That's weird!" Sal exclaimed. "It's not storming. I wonder what's going on? Come on, let's tell Mom!" We both ran up the stairs to the kitchen.

"Did the lights just go off and on up here?" Sal asked his mother.

"No," said Mrs. Martelli. "Why do you ask?"

Sal explained about the lights going off and on in the basement, and Mrs. Martelli said, "The light bulb is probably just loose. Let's go screw it in tight." She went back downstairs with us, and we saw that the basement lights were on, just like we left them. Mrs. Martelli flipped the switch off, wrapped a towel around her hand, and tried the light bulb. "It seems to be in tight," she said. "Maybe it's getting ready to burn out."

"Yeah, I guess so," said Sal. So, we went up to Sofi's room, where she and Ollie had about a hundred books scattered out all over the floor. "Look at this killer book about pirates!" gushed Ollie. "I wish I had it."

"You better get them all put away," I told him. "Come on, we've gotta go so Mom can take us to get our new soccer shoes for this year."

A FEW DAYS LATER Mom went with Ollie and me to visit the Martellis after dinner. Ollie and I went to the family room with Sal and Sofi while Mom talked to Mrs. Martelli in the kitchen.

"Well, we're going to Konza," said Sal. "Mom took us to enroll, and I'm gonna be in Mr. Franklin's home room. I've never had a man for a teacher before." He admitted he was a little nervous.

"Don't worry," I said. "I'll show you my Konza yearbook from last year and you can see pictures of the kids who'll be in your class."

The last day of summer vacation, we all rode our bikes to the Indian Mission. While Sofi tried to teach Ollie how to do headstands against the wall, Sal and I talked about the new school year.

"I've heard Mr. Franklin is hard in math," I told Sal. "I'm glad I'm going to be in Ms. Patel's class."

"I'm not worried about math. I just want to get started. I'm tired of wondering what it will be like, and feeling like I don't belong here yet, but I'm not in New Jersey anymore either. You know what I mean?"

"Uh, not really, I've lived in the same house all my life. Don't you like your new house?"

"Yeah—mostly." He hesitated, and looked over his shoulder to make sure Sofi and Ollie weren't listening. "If I tell you something, do you promise not to tell anyone else, not even your parents?" I wasn't sure what to expect—some secret about a girlfriend back in New Jersey or something?—but I promised. He said, "Well, a couple of days ago I was in the basement, and you know that room behind the water heater, where Butterscotch was barking?" I nodded, and he went on, "I thought for sure I heard something moving in there. So I went to look, but I didn't see anything."

"Maybe there really is a mouse," I suggested. "Sometimes squirrels even get in houses."

"Maybe," said Sal. "But then yesterday I took some boxes downstairs for my mom, and I heard it again. I still didn't see anything in there, except for the stuff we're not using now, so I set the boxes on the floor right inside the door, and stacked them up against the wall, real straight so they wouldn't fall over. Then on my way back upstairs, I heard the boxes fall over. So I went back, and they were all over the floor!"

"So they fell over. Are you sure you didn't kick them by accident when you left?" I asked.

"No, I was super careful! Anyway, I just left them that way, but here's what's really weird—I went down there again a little later, and get this—the boxes were all stacked up again! Only they weren't stacked in the same order as before. I put the biggest one on the bottom, but it was on top of another one when I went back."

"Your mom or dad probably stacked them back up."

"No, it was only like an hour later. Dad was at work and Mom was busy in the kitchen…that's why she asked me to take them down. And remember, that's where the lights went off and on, too."

"Yeah, but your mom said the bulb might be burning out. Somebody else just moved the boxes after you went back upstairs. There's nothing weird about that," I said.

"Yeah, I guess that makes sense." He gave me an embarrassed look. "Just don't tell anyone about it, OK?"

On the way home we stopped to see our next-door neighbors, Wally and Betty Howard. They're both retired and they've lived in their house like forty years. They probably know everything that's ever happened in Fairway. Betty opened the door before we even knocked and said, "Good timing—you must have known I was baking cookies this morning."

"That's not why we came," I said, but Ollie said, "Awesome!" She took us to the kitchen, where snickerdoodles were cooling on a rack. This was the first time Sal and Sofi had been in the Howards' kitchen, and they looked around curiously. A gray- and black-striped cat was napping in the corner.

"That's Mephistopheles," said Betty. "He likes to have his tummy rubbed."

We always called Betty by her first name. She used to be a teacher, and said she had been called 'Mrs. Howard' for thirty-five years, so she didn't mind us calling her by her own name. She had taught fifth grade, and talked to Sal and me about the things we would do in the new school year, while Sofi and Ollie played with Mephistopheles.

Wally asked Sal and Sofi what they liked to do, and about their move from New Jersey. They're always real nice to kids. Their grandkids live in St. Louis, so they don't get to see them all the time, but they treat Ollie and me almost like their own.

"What's your favorite subject in school?" Betty asked Sal and Sofi.

"Math," said Sal.

"Gym," said Sofi.

They already know my favorite subject is art, and Ollie's is science.

"Tomorrow's a big day for you," said Wally. "First day in a new school. Are you ready?"

I could tell talking to Betty was making Sal feel better about it. "I think so," he said.

"I think you'll really like Konza," said Betty. "You can stop here after school any time you want, if your mother is at work."

Chapter 4

Runaway Marbles

By the first week of September, everyone was busier than ever. Sal's mom got a job at the hospital. Sofi started a gymnastics class and Sal signed up for soccer. Ollie and I re-joined our old soccer teams. My friends Mady and Taylor and I all signed up for band class. I wanted to learn to play flute, and Mady and Taylor decided to try clarinet. Sal and I were in different home rooms and mostly went our separate ways at school, but we still usually walked home together with Ollie and Sofi.

On the way home one afternoon in early September, I asked Sal about the accelerated math class Mr. Franklin was going to teach after school. To get into the class, you had to pass an exam. Sal already had a reputation as a rock star in math and was a lock to get in, but I hadn't decided whether I should take the exam.

"Why not?" Sal asked. "You either make it or you don't—you might as well try."

"I know. Mom and Dad said I should do it. Mom's an accountant, and she says girls are just as good at math as boys."

"You think so?" cut in Sal.

"Uh…*yeah*!" I gave his shoulder a shove. "I guess I'll have to just prove it to you!"

I was ready for him to argue back that boys were smarter than girls, but he seemed to be thinking about something else. "Why're you so quiet? What's up?" I asked.

Sal looked back to see if Ollie and Sofi were listening. Ollie was throwing his backpack in the air and trying to catch it, while Sofi tried to knock it out of his hands.

"So…remember when I told you about the boxes I took to the basement that got scattered on the floor?" Sal asked.

I nodded. "I haven't told anyone about it, not even Ollie."

"I know we decided there was probably nothing weird going on, but something else happened. It's been cool at night, right? I opened the window in my room to let some fresh air in last night. And sometime in the night I heard the window snap shut! I opened my eyes, and I had this funny feeling like there was someone standing by my bed. But then I figured it was just a dream, so I went back to sleep. But when I got up this morning, the window was closed."

"It's probably just loose. We have some windows in our house that we have to prop open with a stick, 'cause they won't stay open," I said.

"But it's not loose. It was hard for me to open it. I don't see how it could have slipped."

"So what do you think it was then—a ghost?" I laughed. I was starting to wonder if Sal took the ghost stuff *way* too seriously. After all, he was *barely* ten. You know how some kids will believe anything you tell them.

"Well…haven't you ever heard of a haunted house?" he asked.

"Yeah, they're those scary places you go at Halloween where zombies jump out at you and scare you half to death! Mom and Dad won't let us go."

"No, I don't mean Halloween stuff—you told me yourself that things have happened in this neighborhood. And I've read about haunted houses on the internet."

I thought Sal was really going over the edge, but I didn't say it. "My mom says the ghost stories are baloney. Everything you told me about could have happened for a normal reason! If you're so scared, maybe you should go tell your mom and dad," I suggested.

"No way!" he said. "I'm not scared, and anyway, Mom would think I'm crazy, and then she'd say I'm spending too much time on the internet, and lock me out of the computer. No, thanks! I've just never had anything like this happen to me before."

"Well, we could ask Wally and Betty. They've lived in the same house forever, and they would know if anything strange has happened around here," I said. I was sure Wally and Betty would tell Sal—in a nice way, of course—to get his head examined.

So, we sent Sofi and Ollie on home, and knocked on the Howards' door. Sal explained to Wally that he had a special problem he needed to discuss with someone. Betty joined us, and Sal told them about the boxes falling over and the window slamming shut. I thought they would smile and kindly tell Sal that weird things always have a logical explanation—like my mom says—so I was super surprised at what they said next.

"Well, there have been rumors as long as I can remember about ghosts in this area," said Wally. "Supposed to be spirits of Indians—Native Americans—who lived around here years ago. You know, a number of tribes came to Kansas from other states when the government wanted their land for settlers. Shawnee, Wyandot, Delaware—they were all here."

"Did you ever hear that strange things happened in *our* house before?" asked Sal.

"Not specifically," answered Wally. "But I do remember one family that lived there, oh, maybe thirty years ago, who moved out in a hurry. They had a couple of kids in school, and we were surprised that they only stayed a few months. We never knew why they left."

I'd never heard about that before, and I have to admit I was interested.

Betty added, "My mother used to tell me about the rumors of ghosts around the old Shawnee Indian Mission. I haven't thought about those stories in years."

"What did the ghosts do?" asked Sal.

"Oh, nothing really harmful, just annoying, like spilling pitchers of milk and knocking books off shelves," said Betty.

Sal looked at me. "Or knocking over boxes and closing windows?"

"Exactly," said Wally. "So you see, you're not the first person to wonder about things that seem strange around here."

"But do you believe the rumors?" I asked. I wondered if Betty and Wally were just trying to make Sal feel better.

"Well," said Betty, "you know they've had ghost hunts at the Mission, but I've never heard of anyone actually seeing one."

Sal perked up. "A ghost hunt? I want to go on one of those!"

"I'm pretty sure it's for adults only, or at least older

kids," said Wally. "But I don't think your house is haunted. If it was, we surely would have heard about it by now."

"I guess you're right," said Sal. "And please don't tell my mom."

As we got up to leave, I had another thought. "Betty, Mr. Franklin's going to teach an accelerated math class after school this year. Do you think I should take the entrance exam?"

"I don't know why not," answered Betty. "There's nothing mysterious about math, and we all use it every day in ways we don't even think about. If you don't try new things, you'll never know how good you might be at something."

So, I SIGNED UP to take the math exam, which was in a week. I worked extra hard on the daily math homework, and asked Sal to explain some problems I had a hard time with. The exam was set for a Thursday after school, and nine boys and seven girls signed up for it. There were fifteen problems on the test, and we had thirty minutes to do them. I felt pretty good about some of the questions, but a few were just impossible! Sal was one of the first ones finished, but I didn't hand in my paper until Mr. Franklin called time. After that I just wanted to get out of there.

When I got to our corner, I saw Sal sitting on the

step leading up to my house. "What did you think?" he asked. He got up and we both headed to his house.

"Boy, am I glad that's over!" I said. "I don't know if I'll pass or not. What about you?"

"It wasn't bad," he replied. "We'll find out on Monday. Anyway, do you want to come in and see how the playroom is coming along?"

We went inside and down to the basement. Mr. Martelli had done a lot of work on the playroom. The space at the bottom of the steps had a big black rubber mat in the center for Sofi to practice gymnastics. There was a wooden balance beam on the mat with some cushions stacked under it. The beanbag chairs were in one corner facing a television. There was even a desk where you could draw or maybe put a computer. Metal shelves along the walls held games, books and toys. It looked like a great place to play when it was too hot or cold to go outside.

Before we turned to go back upstairs, I glanced into the small room behind the water heater. I saw a lumpy bag in a patch of sunlight on the floor, and a few shiny marbles nearby. "Are those your marbles?" I asked.

Sal was already starting up the steps, but turned to look into the room. "What are my marbles doing there? I put them on the bookcase! Sofi must have gotten them out and not put them away!" He gathered up the marbles, replaced them in the bag, and laid the bag on the nearest beanbag chair. "Come on, let's get something to eat."

"Good idea," I said as I followed Sal up the stairs. As I looked over my shoulder at the doorway to the little room, I swear I saw a shadow move across the square of sunlight. But I knew there was nobody there—it must have been the sun going behind a cloud.

Chapter 5

Cheers for Orion

The next Monday morning, I could hardly eat breakfast. All I could think about was whether or not I passed the math test. I wanted to prove that girls could be just as good at math as boys. Of course, I hoped that some other girls would pass the test, too. "Let's go, Ollie!" I said.

"You've still got ten more minutes before you have to leave," said Mom. "Let Ollie finish his breakfast."

"Come on, Ollie, don't be such a slowpoke!" He finally gulped his last bite of Cheerios, and we grabbed our backpacks and ran out the door. I walked as fast as I could to school, making Ollie practically run to keep up. I raced down the hallway to Mr. Franklin's room where a white paper was taped to the wall beside the door. Alex Carter was already there, looking at the paper.

"I'm in!" exclaimed Alex. "And so are you! Luke and Matt, too, and Mady and Taylor."

What a relief! I counted the names on the paper. "Twelve people passed the test! But it doesn't tell us how many we got right, does it?"

I looked in the door and saw Mr. Franklin at his desk, so I went in.

"Congratulations, Orion! You passed the test! I'm looking forward to having you in the class," he said.

"I was wondering if I could see my test paper," I said. "I'd like to know which questions I missed, so I can learn how to do them right."

Mr. Franklin looked at a paper on his desk. "You got ten right out of fifteen," he said. "We'll be going over all the questions in the first class to make sure everyone knows how to work them."

"Thanks!" I called as I ran out the door to my home-room.

I couldn't wait to tell Sal, Wally and Betty—and Mom and Dad. My head was in the clouds the whole day, and Mady, Taylor and I celebrated at recess, shouting "Girl Power!' at all the boys. I wanted school to be out so I could tell Sal how great I felt, but as I started home, I saw him walking ahead with two boys from Mr. Franklin's class, and Ollie was tagging along. *Well, he already knows I made it,* I said to myself. *I'll just talk to him later.*

I went home to tell Mom the good news, and she sent

me to find Ollie. He was still in the Martellis' yard with Sal.

"I passed the math test," I announced to Sal.

"I know—cool!" He gave me a thumbs up, but he and the other boys were tossing a football, and he didn't stop to talk to me, so I told Ollie to get moving and we left. Later that evening at dinner, Dad told me how proud he was of me.

"I'll bet Sal was glad you made it," he said.

That kind of burst my bubble. "He didn't seem very happy for me. He didn't even want to talk to me about it, he just wanted to play football! I thought he'd brag about how many he got right, or something. Do you think he's mad that I made it?"

Ollie snorted. "Nah—he's just freaked because some of the guys in his class said that you're his girlfriend, that's all. Justin and Adam, who were with us after school? Don't worry, I told them no way!"

I could only gasp.

Mom said, "I wouldn't worry about it too much. If anyone asks you, just tell them Sal's your friend and neighbor, and you're both interested in math. It's okay for boys and girls to be friends. Don't get sucked in to any big drama."

The next day at lunch, Taylor, who's in Mr. Franklin's class with Sal, said, "I heard Justin Riggs ask Sal if you're his girlfriend."

"Yeah, I heard about that already," I said. "If anybody asks you, tell them it's not true—you can say it came straight from me!"

"Sure," said Taylor. "Justin's always trying to stir something up. Anyway, Sal told him he was crazy. Pretty soon Justin'll start teasing somebody else."

"Besides," said Mady, "I think Lucy Martin likes him."

"You're kidding!" I almost spit my milk out. "Does he know?"

"Probably," said Taylor. "There aren't many secrets in Mr. Franklin's class."

That evening after dinner I told Mom what I had heard from Mady and Taylor.

"By next week that'll be ancient history," she said. "That's the thing about fifth grade—likes and dislikes change really fast. Has Sal said anything to you about it?"

"No, he's probably too embarrassed."

Just then Ollie came into the kitchen. "Are you talking about Sal and Lucy Martin?" he asked.

"How do *you* know about that?" I asked.

"It's a guy thing," said Ollie. "Dudes know all about it when girls like them."

"Oh, *really*!" I said, rolling my eyes. "Well, you'll never have to worry—no girl's gonna be dumb enough to 'like' you!"

"So what? Anyway, Sal doesn't want a girlfriend right

now. That's why he likes you—you're a good friend even if you are a *girl*."

I threw a wet dishcloth at Ollie's head, but he ducked, and the dishcloth hit the wall and slid to the floor.

"Enough!" said Mom. "Don't you have homework, Orion? And Ollie, time to hit the showers. Off with you!"

Chapter 6

Who Got in the Paint?

Sal seemed to be fitting in really well with the kids at Konza. He was the shortest boy in fifth grade, but nobody gave him a hard time because he was a good athlete and a cool guy. After the day we talked to Wally and Betty about the strange things in his house, he didn't mention any more weird stuff to me.

And I never thought I'd say this, but it was pretty cool to have a boy for a friend. I get along OK with most of the boys in my grade, but I spent a lot of time with Sal because his mom was working day shifts at the hospital a few days a week. He and Sofi usually hung out with us until she got home. Talking to him was a lot different than talking to my girlfriends.

One evening before dinner my mom asked me how

he was getting along in school. I told her he seemed to be just fine.

"The girls like him because he's polite and nice, and the boys like him because he's good at sports and math, but doesn't have a big head," I said.

"I'm glad," said Mom. "You know it was hard for him to move. His mother told me he had to give up being on a select baseball team last summer."

"You mean because they moved?" I asked.

"That, and they just didn't have the money," she said. "Sofi didn't get her gymnastics lessons, either. Sal was pretty upset about it."

"Really?" I said. "He never mentioned that to me. He just said he didn't like leaving his friends and he wasn't sure about going to public school."

"They are such a nice family," said Mom. "I'd hate to think he was having any problems."

"Well…there *is* something I noticed," I said. "He's told me some things that made me wonder if he's a little crazy."

"Like what?" asked Mom.

"Well, Ollie told him about the ghost stories people tell about the Indian Mission, and he took it kinda seriously. And then he said some funny things happened to him at their house."

"Nothing bad, I hope?" asked Mom.

"No!" I said. Then I remembered my promise to Sal that I wouldn't tell anyone—*anyone*—about the things he'd told me. "Just, like, his window slammed shut and he thought there was somebody in his room one night, but he knows he was just dreaming."

"You know those things have nothing to do with ghosts," said Mom, "but sometimes when people are going through a hard time, they say or do things to get attention."

"Well, he hasn't said anything like that for quite awhile. I think he's worked his way through it," I said. "You're not going to tell his mom, are you?" I knew I'd already said too much, and if Sal's mom heard about it, he'd know where it came from.

"No, as long as what he says is pretty harmless," she said. "I just want the whole family to be happy here. They've had a tough time this last year."

I got out of the kitchen as fast as I could. Why did I have to have such a big mouth sometimes? I promised myself I wouldn't say anything else about what happened at Sal's house.

MR. MARTELLI WAS ALM OST finished with the playroom in their basement. It still needed some new carpet, but he'd painted the walls a light color and put up yellow curtains at the windows. There was a big table where you could play board games or do your homework, like a kids-only family room. After what my mom told me, I guessed Sal's parents were trying to make it up to him for having to leave his friends and give up the select baseball team. I went with him after school one afternoon to see how it looked.

"Sofi and I get to paint the walls however we want," he said, and he showed me where he had started painting the background for his Mets logo. He had a color picture of the logo taped to the wall to copy off of. "Maybe I'll do something for football, too. Sofi wants to paint some girls doing gymnastics."

"Wow, I wish my dad would fix up our basement like this!" I said. I looked at the painting. So far it was just a white circle on the wall with blue buildings in the middle, and an orange border around it.

"I'm ready to paint the stitching on the circle," said Sal. "To make it look like a baseball, see? But it's gonna be hard."

"Maybe I could help a little," I said. I love to draw, and I *am* pretty good at it. "We'll just trace the lines in with pencil, real light, then paint over them."

"Oh, great idea!" said Sal.

"Looks like you got some paint on the floor," I said, pointing to some little orange drops.

Sal looked at the floor and said, "Hey! The lid's off my

paint can! I know I put it back on last night!" He got on his knees and looked at the trail of tiny orange drops on the concrete. "And where's my paintbrush?!"

Just then Sofi and Ollie came down the stairs.

"What's all the yelling about?" asked Ollie.

Sal turned on Sofi. "Did you open my paint can?" he yelled. "Somebody took my brush and dripped paint on the floor!"

"It wasn't me!" said Sofi, looking hurt. Sal hardly ever yells at her.

"We just got here," said Ollie. He got down on the floor and put his finger on one of the orange spots. "Hey, it's still wet!" he cried. "Was somebody down here painting while we were at school?"

"No way!" said Sal. "OK, where do the drips go?"

We all got down and started looking for the orange spots. They seemed to lead toward the little room behind the water heater. The door of the room, which was usually wide open, was nearly closed. Sal made a beeline for the door and was about to push it open, when suddenly the door slammed shut!

C-C-CRASH!! At that same moment, a little piggy bank that was sitting on top of a bookcase tumbled down and shattered on the floor. We all stopped in our tracks and looked at each other.

"Let's get out of here!" said Sal, heading for the steps.

We ran upstairs and back across the street to our house as fast as we could.

"Good thing you didn't get your hand caught in that door!" said Ollie as we flopped onto the kitchen chairs.

"Everything OK?" Mom asked as she came out of her office. We looked at each other and giggled while she made a snack for us. Chewing our peanut butter sandwiches, we all calmed down a little.

"Mrs. O'Brien, what could make something fall off the top of a bookcase?" asked Sal. "My piggy bank just fell and broke in the basement, and I didn't even touch it!"

"And a door almost slammed on his hand!" added Ollie.

"Well, you know we have earthquakes here, don't you?" said Mom. "They're not big ones, and most of the time we don't even feel them. But they can cause cracks in the walls of houses. We've got some in our upstairs hall. An earthquake could easily knock a piggy bank off a shelf."

"Could an earthquake make a door slam?" I asked.

"I don't know, but probably," said Mom. "You never know in these old houses."

We took our sandwiches and went out to the front porch. "It probably was just an earthquake," I said. "You know there's always a reason why things happen."

"That part makes sense," said Sal, "but it doesn't explain why the drips of wet paint were on the floor, or why the paint can lid was off."

"Or where your paintbrush went," said Ollie.

"Are you *sure* you closed the paint can?" I asked. "Sometimes I forget to do something, and I can't believe it later. Maybe the phone rang, or your mom called you for dinner."

"Maybe," said Sal. "But I don't remember anything like that."

THE NEXT DAY WAS Thursday, and we had accelerated math after school. As I walked home with Sal afterward, I asked if he had found his paintbrush.

"It was on top of the dryer by the sink," he said. "When I went down after dinner, the lid was on the paint can, too. I guess my mom or dad put it back on. I must have really zoned out about something that day."

"Don't worry about it," I said. "I forgot to put the ice cream carton back in the freezer one day, and it melted all over the counter. Mom made me help clean it up."

"You should have told her Ollie did it," said Sal.

"I didn't think of that," I said. "But next time…. "

Chapter 7

The Festival—and a Surprise

I couldn't believe how fast the year was moving. It was already October, and Ms. Patel was teaching us about mapmaking. I practiced drawing maps of my house, my neighborhood, and the school. I liked the math class, too. Mr. Franklin had a way of explaining solutions to problems that made them seem simple, and he always walked us through the steps we needed to solve them. I was learning my flute fingerings and how to read music. I had my life under control...I thought.

One day after the accelerated math class, I waited for Sal to walk home with me. I wanted to remind him of the Shawnee Indian Mission Festival coming up the next week. But he came out of the classroom with Alex Carter and Josh Goldberg, and they didn't look at me as they went to the door. So I went out to the curb with Mady to wait for her mom to pick her up.

"Did Sal already leave?" she asked.

"Yeah, he just walked out with Alex and Josh," I said. Mady's mother pulled into the circle drive and offered me a ride. When I got home, Sal, Alex and Josh were sitting on the Martellis' front step. I didn't like being ignored, so I went over to see what they were doing.

"This is a boys' thing," said Alex. "No girls allowed."

"So get lost," said Josh.

"Oh, yeah?" I said. "Is that what you say, Sal? It's your house."

"Can't I just be with the guys sometimes?" asked Sal. He didn't sound mean or mad, but he didn't smile or anything. Alex and Josh snickered. What was I supposed to do?

"Fine," I said, and went back home.

"Orion? What's up?" asked Mom as I threw my backpack onto a kitchen chair. She came out of her office. "What's the matter?"

"I was going to tell Sal he could come with me to the Indian Mission Festival next week, but he's over there with Alex and Josh, and they said they don't want any girls around. They told me to get lost!" I was getting pretty worked up.

"Don't be too upset, honey. After all, Sal wants time with other boys, just like you want to spend time with your girlfriends. It doesn't mean he's not your friend anymore," she said.

"But I'd never tell him to get lost just because he's a boy!" I said. "That was just mean!" I got madder by the minute as I complained to Mom. "I've tried to be nice to him ever since he moved here, and now he's acting like a big jerk!"

Mom gave me a hug and said, "Calm down a minute. Did Sal tell you to get lost?"

"No…that was Josh," I admitted. "Sal just said he wanted to be with the boys."

"I know it hurt your feelings, but he just told you the truth. It's OK to spend time with different people. Don't let him know it bothered you. Just leave him alone for a few days, and before you know it, he'll come and want to talk to you."

"What if I don't want to talk to him?" I said.

"Well, nobody can make you talk to him," said Mom. "But then you'd be acting just as mean as those boys. Is that what you want—to hurt his feelings like he hurt yours?"

"I don't know," I said. "Maybe."

"Why don't you take Butterscotch out for a good long walk?" said Mom. "It's a beautiful day and you'll feel better when you get home."

I took Butterscotch clear to the Indian Mission and all the way around the grounds. I thought a lot about what the boys had said and decided Mom was right. I'd just wait until Sal was ready to talk to me again, and not act mad or anything. Even though I kind of was.

AS IT TURNED OUT, Mom and Dad invited the Martellis to go to the Shawnee Indian Mission Festival with us. The Festival always takes place in early October. It starts on a Friday night with a concert, then on the weekend they have Native American dancing, demonstrations of frontier life, people dressed in old-fashioned costumes, and tours of the Mission buildings. You can buy food cooked over campfires like in the old days. It's a great chance for everyone to hang out with friends, eat a lot, and have fun outside.

I hadn't talked to Sal much for the last week, but I walked behind our parents with Sofi to the Mission grounds. Sal and Ollie ran ahead. The concert got started, and we sat on blankets, listening to the music and eating. After we ate, lots of the kids ran around the grounds as it got dark. My mom and dad milled around with the grownups. Sal hung out with a group of boys, and I sat on a blanket with Mady and Taylor.

"You know, Sal *is* pretty cute," said Taylor. "And he's really smart. Are you sure you don't like him? You spend a lot of time together."

"Get serious!" I said. "He lives across the street, and

he and his sister hang out with us when their mom's at work sometimes. Besides, he's too short for me."

"Well, you're taller than *all* the boys in our grade," said Mady.

"So what? He's not my boyfriend, and that's that! And I told you what he and Josh and Alex said to me last week." I couldn't believe my best friends were giving me a hard time about this.

"You know he was just acting like that because he was with the boys," said Taylor. "He's always nice to the girls in our class."

"Hey, I'm not mad at him," I said (yeah, I know, that was a little white lie). "If he wants to talk to me, he can." Right then I saw Ollie running toward our street, and wondered if he was going home early, but decided he wasn't my problem. My friends and I shared some more gossip from our class.

TO UNDERSTAND WHAT HAPPENED next, you have to know why Ollie went home early that night. I didn't find out until later, but, knowing him, it made perfect sense.

As the sun went down at the Festival, it started to get chilly. I'd planned ahead and worn a sweatshirt, but Ollie, as usual, was in a T-shirt. He got cold, so Mom told him he could go home and get a sweatshirt. As he ran past Sal's group of boys, Sal called out to him.

"You leaving already, Ollie?"

"Gotta go home to get my sweatshirt—I'm cold!" Ollie replied.

Sal, who was also wearing a T-shirt, said, "Hey, let me come with you—I'm a little cold, too!"

They ran toward our house, but when they got there, Ollie slapped his forehead. "Oh, no—I forgot to get the key from Mom!"

"Are you serious?" asked Sal. "OK, just come over and get one of mine." Sal had his own key, so the two of them ran over to the Martellis' house. Upstairs, Sal grabbed a sweatshirt for each of them. They ran back down the stairs, and just as they reached the front door, a clattering sound came from the basement.

"What was that?" asked Ollie. "Do you think there was an earthquake?"

"I don't know—maybe the door slamming knocked something off a shelf," Sal replied. "Come on, we'll check." He hit the light switch to the basement stairs and they ran down. At first nothing appeared out of place, but then they saw marbles scattered near the little back room, some still rolling on the floor.

Sal started scooping up marbles. "I wonder how that happened—I left them in the bag on the beanbag chair," he said. Ollie saw the bag on the floor of the little room, and picked it up. He and Sal were grabbing more marbles and stuffing them in the bag, when all of a sudden they stopped short. In the corner, in the shadows near the floor, a face with wide, startled eyes stared at them in the half-darkness.

"WHAA-A-A?!" Both boys yelped in astonishment.

"Who—who are you?!" shouted Sal. He and Ollie stood rooted to the floor. (I would give anything to have seen their faces right then!) In the dim light of the little room, they could make out a head of very black hair falling over dark eyes in a light brown face. A boy was kneeling near the shelves. He looked surprised, but then slowly stood up and faced them.

Chapter 8

The Big Reveal

Back at the festival, I was chilling with my friends. A few minutes after I saw Ollie leave, Mom came over to our blanket and said, "Ollie went home to get a sweatshirt, but he forgot to take the house key. Would you please run after him and give it to him?" She held out the key to me.

"Awww, Mom! Do I have to?" I pleaded. "He won't freeze to death! Maybe that will teach him to take the key with him!"

"Just take him the key and you can come back for a little while. We're going to head home in about a half hour," she said.

I looked at Mady and Taylor with a sigh. "He owes me for this one," I said. "Save my place, and I'll be back."

I ran home with the key, to bail my brother out like

always. When I got there, Ollie wasn't on the front porch as I expected. Where was the little brat? I looked across the street and saw a light on in the Martellis' front hall. Could he be over there? I didn't really want to go see, 'cause I *was* still a teeny bit mad at Sal, but I had to find Ollie. Muttering to myself that I would make him pay for this, I crossed the street to the Martellis' and saw that the door was partly open.

"Ollie?" I called. No one answered, but I could see a light coming from the basement steps. "Yo!" I yelled, and followed the light. Just then I heard both Sal and Ollie yell, "WHAA-A-A?!" It sounded like they were afraid of something. I ran down the steps. Both boys were standing just inside the little basement room, but I couldn't see what had scared them.

"What do you think you're doing, Ollie?" I demanded when I got down the steps. I had *really* had it with him. "Mom made me come and bring you the house key, and you're messing around over here?" I was ready to beat the you-know-what out of him. That's when I realized Sal was talking to someone. I heard him say, "Who— who are you?" When I came up behind him, I saw a dark-haired boy standing in the corner by the shelf. In one hand he held an antique glass marble that had swirls of yellow, red, blue and green running through it.

"Please," said a soft voice, "I wasn't stealing it, I just like to look at the beautiful beads."

"Beads?" said Ollie.

"Give that back! That's a special marble," said Sal. "It was my grandfather's. What are you doing here, and how did you get in?" He held out his hand for the marble.

"I...I live here," said the boy as he handed it over.

"You don't live here," snorted Sal. "*I* live here. How come I've never seen you before?"

The boy looked down. "I mean no harm," he said. "Truly, I live here in this place—right behind that shelf."

"You'd better tell me what you're doing here before I go get my dad," said Sal. "You look like a burglar! He'll call the police and they'll take you to jail!"

"No!" cried the boy. "I just wanted to touch the beads...er, the marbles. If you'll just listen, and not bring your father, I'll tell you why I'm here."

"Sal!" I yelled. "How did he get in here? Let's go get your dad right now!" I started to run for the steps, but Sal grabbed my arm and stopped me.

"Just wait a minute," he said. "There's three of us and only one of him, so let's give him a chance." He turned to face the boy. "Okay, out with it. How did you get here, and how long have you been here?"

The boy looked straight at Sal and began to speak. His voice was quiet but he used his hands a lot, almost like he was acting out what he said.

"I am Samuel Grayhawk. My sister Molly and I went to school at the Shawnee Mission. Molly got a fever, and was put in a special cabin for the sick people. I knew she was dying, but the white elders wouldn't let me go see her. But I tried anyway—I ran out of the Mission workshop and jumped on a horse that was standing nearby. I rode her hard toward the sick cabin where Molly was, but she stumbled and threw me off."

"Are you kidding me?" Sal stared hard at the boy.

"When I hit the ground I knew I was gravely injured. My bones hurt so, it was more painful than anything I ever felt before." He pointed to his ribs. "So I crawled and made my way to a root cellar nearby. It was getting dark and I just wanted to rest and try to regain my strength."

"Hey—are you OK?" asked Ollie. "Did you break some bones?"

The boy continued. "It was dark and warm in the root cellar. I covered myself up and fell asleep." His voice became even more hushed. "And when I woke up, I…I knew I was…dead." His voice was so soft now that we could barely hear him.

Sal was silent for a moment. "You mean, you actually died?"

"He *died?!* Are you all *crazy*?!" I shrieked. "I'm going to get Mom and Dad *now* and tell them you two…"

"SHUT UP!" said Sal, getting in my face. "Just let him talk, will you?" Sal had *never* told me to shut up before, so I knew he meant business.

The boy nodded. "I could see and hear people,

though. I knew they were looking for me. I heard them say that Molly had died, too. I never got to say goodbye to her, or honor her in the tradition of our people."

"Gee, that's awful," said Ollie.

"That's the tallest tale I've ever heard," said Sal. "Why should I believe you?" *Great*, I thought, *maybe he's finally coming to his senses.*

"I will go away right now, and not bother you again," said the boy.

"No, wait!" cried Sal. "I may be crazy, but I want to hear more about you."

"Please," said the boy, "I do not wish to be seen when men and women are about—only children. If your mother and father see me, they will make me go away."

"How come we've never seen you before, if you live here? And how come we can see you if you're dead?" asked Ollie.

The boy swallowed. "I just wish as hard as I can, and then I'm just...here. I do not know how else to explain it," he said. "I get so lonely, and it is comforting to me to feel like I'm still alive...."

"So...you're really a ghost!" cried Ollie. "Wow, this is so awesome!"

"What is *wrong* with you, Sal? You know he can't be for real," I said. "This kid broke into your house and tried to steal your marbles, and you're letting him get away with it? If you won't go get your dad, I will!"

"Don't listen to her! " said Ollie. "Orion's my sister, and she always bosses everybody else around."

Sal turned to me. "Look, Orion," he said, "you can leave if you want. Take Ollie with you, but it's my house, and I want to hear what he has to say."

"*I'm* not leaving!" cried Ollie.

Well, what could I do? The boy didn't seem dangerous or anything, in fact, I think he was scared to death, but he didn't want to show it. If I left, I might never know what was really going on. "So who are you, really?" I asked. "I think you're lying."

"Seriously?" said Sal. "Nobody could make this up!"

The boy swallowed. "Truly, my name is Samuel Grayhawk. My people, the Wendat, came here after the white leader told us to move to a new land, many miles from where I was born. After the journey, a great sickness came to our people and many Wendat died. My mother first, and then my father. My sister and I were sent to the Mission school, and then my sister became ill also. The teachers would not allow me to visit her—perhaps they feared that I, too, would fall ill—but she was all I had left. I jumped on a horse that was tied outside my workshop and started for Molly's cabin, but the horse stumbled and threw me off, and I was killed.

"I am a spirit now," he continued, "because I died that day. But I never found where Molly was laid to rest so I could pay my respects to her. I have to do that before I can join my family in the spirit world."

"But you can see us, right?" asked Sal.

"I can. I love to watch the children, and I marvel at all your wonderful belongings."

"Holy crap!" I cried, suddenly thinking about why we were here. "We were supposed to go back to the Festival! Mom said she and Dad would be home in half an hour. We'd better figure out what we're going to do about him, quick!"

"Right," said Sal. "My parents will be here soon, so you'd better hide, or whatever you do, but can we talk to you again?"

"Maybe," said Samuel. "I long to have some company. I was all alone in the cellar for such a long time. Then this house was built over it. I tried to stay hidden away when men and women were around, because I believed they would not like having a spirit in the house. But children are more understanding, and less fearful. I like to watch the small gray-eyed girl doing her strange dancing."

Ollie looked at Sal. "You mean Sofi? Dancing?" he laughed. "She does gymnastics!" Samuel gave him a blank look.

"Hush, Ollie!" I suddenly felt very protective of Samuel. "You're safe here, we won't tell anyone. Please come back and see us again!"

Samuel thought a moment. "When your mother and father are away, come and rattle the marbles. That way I'll know it is safe to come out. I have to go now." As we watched, he got harder and harder to see, sort of like smoke when it fades away. After a moment, we all ran up the stairs and out the door as fast as we could.

"I. Do. Not. Believe. This," I said on the front porch.

"No kidding," said Sal. "But we can't talk about it now. Here come my mom and dad."

I looked across the street and saw Mom and Dad and the Martellis coming up the sidewalk. Ollie and I tried to hightail it across the street before they saw us.

"I'm telling Mom you said 'holy crap,'" Ollie said as we ran toward our house.

"Yeah? What else are you going to tell her?" I asked. "That there's a ghost in the Martellis' basement?"

BACK HOME, WE HAD to explain why we hadn't come back to the festival. I thought about telling them Ollie had gotten so cold, he wet his pants, but instead I made up a story about helping Sal with the painting in the playroom. I'm pretty sure they didn't believe me. We said we needed to get to bed because we both had soccer games the next morning, and headed upstairs. On the way, I squeezed Ollie's arm and whispered, "As soon as Mom and Dad are asleep, you're telling me *everything*, OK?"

I got into my pajamas and turned out my light, but lay in the dark, my brain racing back over the evening's events. A few minutes after I heard Mom's door close, I tiptoed over to Ollie's room, and he filled me in on what happened before I got there. I didn't think I would ever get to sleep that night—I couldn't stop thinking about what we had seen. A real ghost?! Maybe the next morning, I'd realize this was all a dream.

Chapter 9

Mysteries Solved

On Saturday Ollie and I dragged out of bed in time for our soccer games. I was still so hyped from the night before, I could barely concentrate on my game, and missed a ball coming right to me. I apologized to my teammates and ran to the car as soon as the game was over.

"Are you feeling OK this morning?" asked Mom in the car. "You looked a little slow out there."

"Uh, I didn't sleep very well," I said. "I think I'll go rest up a bit when we get home."

I was heading upstairs to my room when Ollie and Dad got home from his game.

"How did you do?" asked Mom. Ollie shrugged.

"He looked like he was on another planet," said

Dad. "Not his best game." I motioned to Ollie to come upstairs, and pulled him into my room.

"All I could think about was what happened last night!" he said.

"I know…me too," I told him. "But we've gotta try and act normal, OK?"

IN THE AFTERNOON, WE took Sal and Sofi with us to the Indian Mission Festival to see the Native American dancing. This was always one of my favorite parts. The dancers wore colored feathers and leather boots, and some of them had paint on their faces. They did lots of amazing leaps and jumped through hoops. Sofi liked them because they reminded her of gymnasts.

They chanted while they danced, and others played drums. Ollie jumped around to the drumbeat. "I bet that's a war dance!" he cried.

"I wonder if Samuel knows how to do this?" Sal whispered to me as we watched.

After the dancing, we wandered over to the big building where schoolrooms were. Even though I'd been to the Mission lots of times, it had never seemed quite so real to me before. I'd never *really* thought what it would be like to go to school there. The room had long wooden benches and tables, where several kids could sit together. There weren't any bright posters or wall decorations. My classroom at Konza seemed a lot more interesting and fun.

"Just think, Samuel sat right here, in this room!" I said.

"Shhhh!" whispered Sal. "We still haven't told Sofi!"

"Sorry!" I ducked my head. "How are we going to get your parents out of the house so we can see Samuel again?"

"I've been thinking about that…if they leave, I'll call you and you can come over, and we'll try to get him to see us."

That night after dinner I Googled everything I could think of about the Shawnee Indian Mission. I read that Native American children were brought there to live so they could be taught the ways of the white man. They studied English, and the girls learned sewing and cooking, while the boys learned carpentry and farming.

"Ollie, it says here the kids had classes for six hours a day, then they worked on the farm and in the kitchens for five more hours! I always thought they just, you know, went to school there, like we go to Konza," I said.

"Geez," said Ollie, "the Mission sounds like a bad place!"

"Yeah," I said. I also read that people from many Native American groups—they were called nations—in states like Ohio, Michigan and Illinois had been moved west of the Mississippi River. They were promised land that they would get to live on forever, but the promises were all broken. Lots of them, like Samuel's sister, had gotten sick and died. I looked at a map of North America and thought about how far they had come. I was beginning to feel really bad for Samuel.

The next afternoon, on Sunday, Mr. and Mrs. Martelli went out to shop for some new carpet for the playroom. Sal stayed home with Sofi. He called me as soon as his parents had backed out of the driveway. Ollie and I arrived a few minutes later, breathless. We all sat down in the family room.

"Sofi," began Sal, "we need to show you something."

"Some*body*," added Ollie.

"Right," continued Sal. He kneeled down in front of Sofi so he would have her full attention. "There's a boy who lives in the basement. His name is Samuel. He's... he's a ghost."

"Like a Halloween ghost?" asked Sofi.

"More like a spirit," I said, thinking the idea of a ghost might scare her. After all, she was only seven. "You know, like what's inside a real person that makes you *you*. Most of the time we can't see spirits, but we can see Samuel— at least, sometimes."

Sofi grabbed Sal around the shoulders. "Will he hurt us?"

"No, he's not like that! He seems...nice, actually, and he's real polite. The thing is, he won't come out if there's any grownups around. So now that Mom and Dad are away, we want to go and try to see him—but you have to promise not to tell Mom and Dad about him. Do you promise?"

Sofi crossed her heart and nodded, though she still looked scared.

"Don't worry," said Ollie. "He's not scary at all. Just a kid like you and me."

So, we all headed down the stairs to the basement. The bag of marbles lay on the beanbag chair. Sal picked it up and jiggled it so the marbles clinked together. "Samuel?"

"Samuel?" Ollie repeated. "It's me, Ollie! Sal and Orion and Sofi are with me. Can you come out?"

After a few moments, as if by magic, a shadowy shape appeared from behind the shelves. Samuel stood before us, looking toward the doorway. The shock of seeing him that first night had worn off, and I took a closer look at him. He was a bit taller than Sal, and thin, with large eyes that were nearly black. His straight black hair hung over his forehead and ears.

He said something that sounded like 'kway.'

"Kway?" I said.

"That is the Wendat greeting," said Samuel.

"I thought Indians always said 'how,'" said Sal.

"How?" asked Samuel. He shook his head. "I don't understand."

"Well, we say 'hello' or 'hi,'" said Sal. "Anyway, my

mom and dad are gone for a while, so we wanted to talk to you some more."

Samuel looked at Sofi. "It is the dancing girl," he said. He smiled softly, and Sofi smiled back, though she clung to Sal's side.

"You were in my room," she said.

"What!?" exclaimed Sal, turning to her. "You've seen him before? In your room? Why didn't you tell me?"

"I thought I was dreaming," said Sofi. "But now I know it was him."

"You were in my room, too, weren't you?" asked Sal.

Samuel looked down. "I only wanted some company," he said. "I never meant to frighten you."

All of a sudden it hit me. "Butterscotch!" I cried. "Butterscotch knew you were here!"

"Oh, yeah," said Sal. "The day we brought the dog! We couldn't figure out why she was barking—she must have smelled you or something, even though we couldn't see you."

"Yes," said Samuel, "I would not be able to come out and see the children if a dog lived here." He looked a little nervous. "But I haven't seen the dog since that day."

"You don't have to worry," said Ollie. "Butterscotch lives with us, across the street. But she wouldn't bite you."

"She would not hurt me," said Samuel, "but she would raise your suspicions. I did not want her to give me away."

"We'll bring her again so she can get to know you," I said.

"Whoa!" said Sal suddenly. "Did you make the lights go on and off one day?"

"I meant no harm," said Samuel. "But the tall girl—Orion—was coming into the room, and I had to make sure she would not see me."

"You made the lights go off?" cried Ollie. "All right! Can you teach me how?"

"OMG, Ollie," I said. "Get *real*. Seriously, though, how did you do that?"

"Again, I do not know," replied Samuel. "I was desperate not to be seen, and wished for darkness as hard as I could, and that is what happened."

"So, you go to different rooms in the house?" asked Sal.

"Yes…if I think it is safe, such as at night. I knew there were children sleeping upstairs, and I wanted to see them."

"Did you knock over the stack of boxes I put on the floor by the door?" asked Sal.

"I was in a hurry to get behind the shelf when you put them there and I thought you had seen me! And I put them all back where you left them."

"And what about my paint?" asked Sal. "Did you open my can and move my paintbrush?" A lot of the weird things that had happened in Sal's basement were suddenly making sense.

"I liked the color of the paint, and wanted to see it," said Samuel. "I thought I could put the lid back on before anyone saw me, but you came into the room and I had to get out of sight. I had the brush in my hand, and I got paint on my fingers. As soon as you went away, I put the lid back on."

"Whoa!" said Sal. "You went in the back room, and when I started to open the door, you pushed it shut, right? And the door slamming made my piggy bank fall off the bookcase."

Samuel hung his head. "I'm sorry about the broken… what did you call it? A pig bank?" Then he looked up and said, "Perhaps I can fix it for you."

"Hey, it's OK," said Sal. "Now I know what happened, and I know I'm not crazy."

Just then the telephone rang.

Chapter 10
All About Samuel

_____

"**P**orca vacca!" said Sal. "What if it's Mom calling from the carpet store? I better answer it."

"What does that mean?" asked Ollie as Sal ran upstairs.

Sofi just shrugged, and said, "He never says it around Mommy."

Sal was back in a minute. "It was the hospital. Mom needs to call them when she gets home."

We got back to the business of talking to Samuel. We had so many questions, and we had to ask them before Mr. and Mrs. Martelli got home.

"Why can we see you sometimes, and other times you disappear?" I asked.

"The only way I can explain is to say that when I am lonely, I want so much to be alive again, and I can somehow be like I am now, when you can see me. It makes me feel happy and I want to explore the house and talk to the children I see. But it takes a lot of my strength to do that."

"Are you hungry?" asked Ollie. "We can bring you something to eat."

"No," replied Samuel, "I don't get hungry, or thirsty, or cold. But I do *feel* things—inside—like sadness, because I didn't get to say goodbye to my mother and father and Molly."

"Oh," said Ollie, "now I see why Butterscotch couldn't hurt you."

"So, tell us about coming to live at the Mission," said Sal. We all sat down on the floor, gathered around Samuel.

"I came to the Mission when I was nine summers," Samuel began. "My sister Molly was thirteen. She had to sleep in the girls' room, so I didn't always get to see her, but after supper I could talk with her. I was so lonely for my mother and father, I wanted to be with Molly so we could talk about how it was when our family lived together."

"But you said your parents died," said Sal. "Is that why you went to the Mission?"

"Many children were brought to live at the Mission school. I wanted to stay with my grandparents, but they told me I must learn the white man's ways. We were sad to leave our families, but at least I had Molly. When we were alone, we could speak our own language, and I loved hearing her tell me the stories of our people. But the white teachers told us we had to speak English, and learn to live like they did, and to forget the ways of our own people."

"That's terrible!" I said. "Were they mean to you?"

"They were harsh, not kind and loving like our mothers and fathers. They punished us if we did not speak and act the way they wanted," said Samuel. "They told us they were trying to help us, but I did not believe them. They did not respect us, and looked down on our customs and manners."

"Nobody likes to be dissed," said Sal.

Samuel gave him a blank look. "My people respect everything—the earth, skies, animals, and other people, even those who are different from us."

"Who were your people, exactly?" asked Sal. "What were they like?"

"The Wendat," answered Samuel. "I was from the Deer clan. My grandmother was a clan mother, and my father was a leader among the people."

"Did you live in a teepee?" asked Ollie.

"What is a teepee?" asked Samuel. "Oh, I know—I have heard of those, but have never seen one. We lived in long houses made of trees and bark. Many of our kinsmen lived there with us."

"What are kinsmen?" asked Ollie.

"My family—my mother and father, and my mother's father and mother, and her brothers and their wives and children—we all lived together."

"And did you have a tomahawk and fight in wars?" Ollie asked excitedly.

Samuel gave him a funny look. "Do you mean a war club?" he asked. "The Wendat were known as fearless warriors when they defended their homes and villages. But since I was born, my people have lived in peace with all nations."

"So how old are you now?" asked Sal. "I mean, how old were you when you died?"

Sofi gasped. "He *died*!?" She looked on the verge of crying.

"Do not be afraid, Little Gray Eyes," Samuel said. "Yes, I was thrown from a horse when I tried to go see my sister, who was very, very sick. I was wounded badly, so I crawled under a gunnysack in the root cellar to keep warm and rest. My wounds were so bad that my body died, but my spirit stayed here, at this place. Most of the time I stay hidden from the people who live in the house, but I am so lonely…when I see children, I want to come out and join them."

"What's a gunnysack?" asked Sal.

Samuel looked at him. "Just…a gunnysack, to keep potatoes and onions in."

He continued, "I was eleven in the Strawberry Moon before my fall. Molly was fifteen summers when she got the sickness."

"The Strawberry Moon?" I asked.

"Yes, the moon when the strawberries ripen," answered Samuel. Sal shrugged.

"So, you had a big sister, too," said Ollie. "Did she boss you around all the time?"

"My sister was a guide and example for me," said Samuel. "Sisters are very important for the Wendat. They help their brothers learn how to be good men. Molly was always patient and kind with me."

"Geez, I wish my sister was like that!" said Ollie.

"Yeah, well, I wish my brother was like Samuel!" I said.

"Knock it off, you two!" said Sal. "So why did you stay here, instead of going wherever the others went when they died?" he asked Samuel.

"I do not know, really," said Samuel. "But I—that is, my *spirit*—cannot let go of this place until I find where Molly was laid to rest. The Wendat believe that when we die we should be buried with the people we know and love. Maybe when I find her, I can join her."

"Have you been trying to find her, all this time?" I asked.

"At first I tried to listen to people talking about what

was happening, and that is how I learned that Molly had died and that people were looking for me. I hoped I would hear someone talk about where they had taken her. But then the Mission closed and all the children and teachers went away. For a very long time there was no one around, but finally this house was built over the cellar where I was hiding. I kept hoping I would meet someone who could help me."

"Did you meet other kids who lived in this house before?" I asked.

"Did I meet any…what?" Samuel looked confused.

"Kids—uh, you know, children," said Sal.

"Two times," replied Samuel. "By then I had discovered that if I concentrated my strength very hard, I could appear as I did when I was alive. The first time, a little girl with blue eyes and white hair saw me when she came down the steps to put away some jars of food. She did not really talk to me, but only smiled. And then, much later, two boys saw me and talked to me. I was so excited to have some other children around, but I only got to see them a few times. I believe their mother heard them talking to me and soon after that, they went away."

I looked at Sal. "That must be the family that Wally told us about," I said.

"So, can you go out of the house?" asked Ollie.

"I have not tried," said Samuel. "In my true spirit

form, when you cannot see me, I am tied to this place where I was when I died. But when I appear to you, like now, I can move around just like when I was alive.

"But I would not wish to leave this house. I cannot risk people seeing me, so I only appear when I think it is safe to be seen. And I know that the world outside the house is much different than it was when I came to the Mission school. So many houses were built. So many different people. I look out the window here"—he pointed to the basement window—"and I see strange things. Strange wagons that have no horses or oxen to pull them but go by themselves. And here in the house—the shiny metal boxes that clean the clothing." He pointed to the washer and dryer. "The candles in those little glasses on the ceiling—they make light without a flame! And the most unbelievable thing of all—the box where people move around inside, so we can see what they are doing, but it seems they cannot see or hear us."

"The television!" cried Ollie. "It's nothing to worry about—those are just moving pictures."

"Moving pictures?" said Samuel.

"It's…hard to explain," I said, "So, when did you come to the Mission? What year?"

"The white teachers taught us that it was 1843," said Samuel. "The white chief was Mr. Tyler."

"Wow—1843!" exclaimed Ollie. "Think how old he is now!"

"The *white* chief? Oh, you mean the president?" asked Sal. I told myself we'd need to look up who was president in 1843.

"You don't look over a hundred years old!" I said.

"You see me as I was the day I died," explained Samuel. "I cannot change now."

"Can we touch you?" I asked. "I mean, you seem so *real*!"

Samuel reached his hand out to me, and I brushed his fingers. They felt cold and dry and not quite real, not like a regular person's hand. It made me shiver. Ollie, Sal and Sofi all took their turn touching Samuel's hand.

"When I gather the strength to be seen, I almost feel like when I was alive. I can touch the things I see around me, and you can touch me.

"I will go now," said Samuel. "I am losing my strength. But I will talk with you again. Please come only when your mother and father are away." And with that, Samuel faded into the shadows. Sal put the marble bag back on the beanbag chair and everyone went upstairs.

"Remember, Sofi, it's a secret—you can't tell *anyone*," reminded Sal.

"I won't tell!" Sofi promised.

Chapter 11

Wally and Betty Help Out

We went straight to the computer. We Googled "Wendat" and learned that it was a form of the name we know as "Wyandotte."

"It's like Wyandotte County," I told Sal and Sofi. "That's right next to where we are. My grandma and grandpa live there, so I've been there a lot."

"Let's see who was president in 1843," said Sal. He Googled "U.S. president 1843" and found, sure enough, it was John Tyler.

Sal was worried that his parents would be home soon. "What are we going to do about him?" he asked. "We can't tell our parents, so we can only go see him when they're gone. I don't want him to be lonely all the time and think we don't care about him!"

"You're right," I said. "We'll have to take every chance we get to see him."

MONDAY AFTER SCHOOL, SAL and Sofi showed up at our door and we all headed up to my room, where Ollie joined us.

"Guess what?" said Sal. "I asked my mom when our house was built, and she said in the 1940s. That means Samuel was in that cellar, or wherever he really was, for at least a hundred years before he ever talked to another person!"

"No wonder he's so lonely," said Ollie. "And all that time, he never knew what happened to Molly!"

"We need to find out more about the Wyandot people, so we can understand what was going on with them," said Sal. We looked on the internet at first, and found a lot of websites with long pages of small print, so we decided to go ask the Howards to explain things to us.

"Mom!" I called. "We're going next door to see Betty! We want to show her what we're doing in math class!"

My mom poked her head out of the office doorway. "Who is 'we?'" she asked. "I didn't realize Ollie and Sofi were doing accelerated math."

"Oh, we're working with them on little kid math," I answered.

Ollie stuck out his tongue, making sure Mom didn't see him.

"Just be sure you're not pestering Wally and Betty. Don't stay too long."

"We'll be polite, I promise. I won't let Ollie beg for cookies or anything," I said. "Remember," I warned as we ran out the door, "we can't give Samuel's secret away, so don't say anything that would make Betty and Wally suspicious."

Sal rang the doorbell and Betty answered. "Hi," I said. "We're trying to learn some more about the Shawnee Indian Mission school. We thought you and Wally might be able to help us."

"What's on your mind?" asked Wally as we sat at the kitchen table and Betty passed around chocolate chip cookies.

"You know how the Indian kids a long time ago came to the Mission school here?" I said. "Well, we met a…a person…whose family moved here back then. He's a Wyandot Indian." I hesitated, unsure how to talk about Samuel without giving away his secret.

"Oh, his ancestors went to school there? I'll bet he can tell you all kinds of interesting stories," said Wally.

"Well, not really," said Sal. "His parents are dead, and he doesn't have a computer or anything to look up stuff. We thought we could help him find out about the Wyandots."

"Oh, you mean he's adopted?" asked Betty.

"Well…not exactly," I said. "We don't really know a

lot about him, but he's our friend and we want to help him. Could you help us find out what happened to the Wyandots in Kansas?"

Wally turned on the computer and after a few minutes found some history of the Wyandots. He read to us that they had originally lived in eastern Canada, and later moved to Ohio and Michigan on the Great Lakes.

"Looks like they came in the early 1840s to the area where the Kansas and Missouri Rivers meet. That was before Kansas was even a state," said Wally. "It says many of the people died in epidemics of typhoid fever and measles. Some of them were buried in a cemetery in Kansas City, Kansas, especially for them. Later most of the Wyandot Nation moved to Oklahoma."

"My teacher told us that the white people just took away all the Indians' land, and kept pushing them farther and farther west. Is that why they came here?" asked Sal.

Wally nodded. "White settlers from Europe wanted land for farming and for building towns and cities. The government made deals with the Indians to move them away from their homelands so white settlers could move in."

"They signed treaties that promised the Indians they could live on the new lands forever," said Betty, "but unfortunately, as more white people moved in, they broke the promises and took that land, too."

"That's terrible!" I said.

"So where did they go?" asked Ollie.

"Many of them ended up on tracts of land called reservations," said Wally. "But they were no longer free to live wherever they wanted. Eventually white people settled the whole country."

"Why did they make the Indian kids go to school and work at the Mission?" asked Ollie.

"A lot of Indian families wanted their children to learn to get along with white people," said Betty. "They thought going to school at the Mission would help them."

"But after the Civil War," said Wally, "the government opened schools and forced the children to go there."

"They actually took them away from their families," said Betty.

We all looked shocked. "That was so mean!" said Sofi.

"I don't think the people who did that thought they were being mean," said Wally. "That was in the nineteenth century, after all. A lot of people thought the Indians were uncivilized, and that if they took their children away when they were young, the children would forget about their Indian ways." He paused a moment. "Attitudes have changed a lot since then. Now we realize how cruel and insensitive that was."

"Insensitive?" asked Sal.

"Some Americans, that is, white people, thought they

were helping the Native American peoples learn a better way of life. They didn't understand that you can't force someone to change the way they've been living for thousands of years just like that. Just think, what if the government made your family move far away, learn a new language, and do jobs you had never done before? You'd be scared, and confused, and very angry."

"The worst thing would be taking kids away from their families, who loved them!" said Ollie. "I would hate it if someone did that to me!"

"Of course, you would," said Betty. "And imagine if someone told you to forget all the stories your parents and grandparents have told you, and the memories you've shared. All your family traditions that make you feel like you belong. You wouldn't feel like yourself any more. That's what the government tried to do to those Indian children." She reminded us that it had happened to thousands of Indian families.

"They didn't respect them," I said.

"They certainly didn't," said Betty.

"Hey," said Sal. "Do you know what a gunnysack is?"

Wally laughed. "I haven't seen a gunnysack in years, but people used to use them all the time. They were just big rough cloth bags used for storing corn seed, or potatoes, or anything else. People even made clothes out of them when times were bad."

Sal looked at the clock. "We'd better be going," he said. "Thanks for the cookies, and for helping us." We all trooped toward the front door.

"Oh, I almost forgot—what's the Strawberry Moon?" I asked.

Wally turned back to the computer screen and typed in another search. "The Strawberry Moon—looks like that means June," he announced.

"June!" exclaimed Sal. "That's my birthday too!"

"What's the moon for February?" I asked.

"And May?" asked Ollie.

"Hold on, let's see here," said Wally. "February—that's the Snow Moon. May? Looks like that's the Flower Moon. And when is your birthday, Sofi?"

"April 14," answered Sofi.

"So, you were born in the Egg Moon," said Wally. "Well! We've learned some very interesting things from your friend."

Out on the sidewalk, Sal said, "That means that Samuel is just a year older than me—I mean he *was*, when he was alive."

"Wally said there was a special cemetery for the Wyandots," I said. "What if Molly is buried there? I wonder if we could find her grave?"

"We'd better tell Samuel about it," said Sal. "He has a right to know where his sister might be."

Chapter 12

Life at the Mission School

$\mathbf{I}$t's funny, but meeting Samuel kind of made things right between Sal and me. If he was with other boys, I didn't butt in, and Sal hung out with Ollie and me just like he had before that day with Josh and Alex. I think we all knew we had a special thing, sharing the secret about Samuel.

We talked to Samuel every chance we got, even if only for a few minutes. One day, after he'd had a chance to get comfortable with us, we took Butterscotch to see him.

"I wish Samuel lived in *our* basement," Ollie complained as we walked Butterscotch across the street after school. "Then we could see him whenever we want."

"Yeah, except that our mom works at home, so we'd probably *never* get a chance to be alone with him," I replied. "We're lucky we can see him when Mr. and Mrs.

Martelli are at work." Sal opened the door as soon as we stepped onto the porch, and we took Butterscotch straight to the little room in the basement with us. She started to whimper, so Ollie and Sofi sat on the floor on each side of her, hugging her to keep her calm. Sal rattled the marbles. "Samuel?" he called. "Can you come out?"

Butterscotch started to growl. "Quiet, girl," said Ollie, patting her gently. She didn't bark, but Samuel didn't come out from behind the shelf.

"Please come out, Samuel," said Sofi as she petted and hugged Butterscotch. "It's OK, Butterscotch won't hurt you. She wants to be your friend. Come and meet her." After a moment, Samuel appeared from behind the shelves. His eyes were on Butterscotch, who kept growling but didn't move. After a moment, Samuel got down on his knees and held his hand out to her. Butterscotch looked at him. She stopped growling and cocked her head to one side, then stretched forward and licked his hand. Samuel broke into a big smile, and Butterscotch wagged her tail as he scratched her ears.

"I had a dog once," said Samuel. "I called him Little Bear because he had black, thick fur, and I took him with me when I went hunting. I raised him from a pup, but he got lost on the journey from our old home."

"I'm sorry you lost him," I said. "But Butterscotch loves you, I can tell. You can see her whenever you want." And sure enough, Butterscotch kept licking Samuel's face and hands, and wagging her tail.

After a few visits, Samuel relaxed a lot. He talked and laughed with us. It was fun telling him about the modern world. One afternoon I brought the Amazon Fire down to the basement. "I found some Native American dances on YouTube. You can watch them on my Amazon Fire," I said.

"*Your* Amazon Fire?" said Ollie. "You mean *our* Amazon Fire—it's mine too!"

I glared at him. "So?" I played a video for Samuel of a Native American hoop dance. The performers wore really fancy outfits, with feathers of all colors on their heads, backs and arms. They stepped in and out of the hoops, swung them over their heads, and threw them into the air. Samuel watched closely, and then asked, "What is this dance? It is not Wendat."

"How do you know?" asked Sal.

"There are some things like our dances, but I cannot tell the meaning of this one."

"You mean every tribe had its own kind of dances?" asked Ollie. "I never knew that!"

"Can you dance like that?" asked Sal.

"Those dancers are very skilled," said Samuel. "I have not done this one, but I am sure I could do it if I practiced."

Samuel was wowed by the computer, but also kind of

suspicious. He wasn't sure if the spirit inside it was good or bad. Ollie told him that the computer was one of the best things ever, but sometimes people do bad things with it.

One time we turned on the television to show Samuel some of the shows we liked. He was fascinated by how it worked, but he didn't really understand any of the programs. Ollie thought it was strange that he never laughed at the funny things, even the cartoons. He just didn't seem to "get it."

"Remember that time we saw some really old cartoons on TV—the ones with the old-style Mickey Mouse?" I reminded him. "They were really stupid, and not funny."

"Do you think that's how Samuel feels about our TV shows?" asked Ollie.

"Probably," I answered. "He's just too polite to say so."

Another thing Samuel thought was really strange was clothes with words and pictures on them. One day Ollie wore his Kansas City Royals T-shirt with a picture of Salvador Perez. Samuel couldn't understand why you would have writing on your shirt.

"Well," I said, "it would be like you wearing a shirt that said 'Wendat' on it. Then everyone would know that was something important to you."

Samuel thought for a minute, then said, "I think I see. We always knew who people were by the way they cut their hair, or how many feathers they wore, or the style of their clothing. I guess it is not so different to have writing on your shirt."

Another day when Sal was wearing a Spiderman T-shirt, Samuel asked if Spiderman was a real person. Sal said that Spiderman was a character in a story that someone made up. He told him some things that Spiderman could do, but explained that he wasn't real.

"My people told stories about magical creatures—the people and animals who created the world we live in, and gave us gifts of corn and fire," said Samuel. "They did amazing things that are not possible now. Our parents and grandparents told us the stories, just as their parents told them."

SAMUEL TOLD US LOTS of things about his life at the Mission school. "We got up very early, before the sun was even up. After breakfast we did some chores—we made our beds, carried water from the well to the kitchen, and brought in firewood. Then we went to the schoolroom where we learned to read and write English. We stayed there all morning, until time for dinner."

"You mean lunch?" asked Sal.

"We had dinner in the middle of the day after our morning lessons," answered Samuel. "Then after that we went to our practical training."

"Did you like school?" I asked.

"The reading was difficult for me," said Samuel. "There

were many words I didn't know the meaning of, and I had to learn what they meant before I could understand what I was reading. It seemed to go so slowly sometimes. But the arithmetic was easy."

"What's arithmetic?" asked Sofi.

"That's what they used to call 'math,'" said Sal.

"You speak good English," I said.

"We were not allowed to speak our own languages," said Samuel. "If the teachers heard us, we would be punished. But sometimes when I sat with Molly after supper, we whispered to one another in the Wendat language. She encouraged me to be strong and not allow the white teachers to make me angry."

"Those teachers were so mean!" said Sofi.

"I tried hard to learn the white man's ways," said Samuel. "I did not wish to bring shame to my people. And I learned many good things. My favorite part of school was the practical training. I was training to be a carpenter in the woodshop. We worked with tools and built furnishings for the Mission buildings. And I used to whittle by the firelight after supper when it was cold outside." His face lit up as he talked about it.

"What's whittling?" asked Ollie.

"It's like carving out of wood," explained Sal. "I've seen some awesome things that people whittle—like duck decoys and things—and they look real!"

"You know what?" I said. "I think there are some old pieces of wood lying around in our basement. I'll bring some for you to whittle!"

"What's he going to do it with—his fingernails?" said Ollie.

"You are such a pain in the butt," I said. "But you're right, he needs a knife."

"I think there's an old pocketknife in our kitchen drawer," said Sal. "I'll look for it as soon as I go upstairs."

By the next afternoon, we had collected two small blocks of wood and a folding pocketknife, which Sal had sharpened on his mom's kitchen sharpener. Samuel examined the wood, which was dark and dusty. "It looks like pine. I'm sure I can make something out of it," he said.

We also took some books to the basement, thinking Samuel might like to read them during the long hours when we couldn't be with him. We found out right away that he couldn't read Sal's books. It wasn't that he couldn't sound out the words. He just didn't understand what the books were about, like sports, and space travel and stuff. We finally brought him some of Sofi's books about animals, with lots of pictures. Those seemed pretty easy for him to read, and he liked looking at the pictures.

Ollie brought Sofi's pirate book to show Samuel, because it was his favorite. There was a picture in it of a ship flying a black Jolly Roger flag, the one with a skull and crossbones. Samuel asked if they put dead people on the ship.

"I don't think so," said Sal. "I think it was just supposed to warn other ships that they were bad guys. Then you could get ready to fight, or you could try to run away."

"I see," said Samuel. "You would not have to wonder if the ship was a friend or an enemy—you would know right away."

I'd never thought about it that way before. I decided Samuel was pretty smart about a lot of things.

Chapter 13

Dressing Like a Wendat

One day, as it got closer to Halloween, Ollie asked Samuel, "Did you ever go trick-or-treating?"

"Tricky treaty?" asked Samuel. "What is that?"

"Trick-or-treating," said Sal. "It's what we do at Halloween. Do you know what Halloween is?"

He had no clue, so we tried to explain.

"We dress up in costumes—you know, to make us look like something or somebody else—and then we go from door to door and ask for candy," I said.

"And what is candy?" asked Samuel.

"You know, sweets...chocolate...sugar?" said Sal. "Stuff we love to eat!"

Samuel gave us a blank look, then said, "You beg for food? And you wear clothing to make you look like someone else? Why would you do this?"

"It's just for fun," I said. "Everybody does it!"

"You can dress up like an animal, or a character from a story, or whatever you want," said Sal.

"I'm going to be Princess Elsa," said Sofi. "I want to wear her beautiful dress!"

"I have an idea!" said Ollie. "I can go as an Indian!"

Everyone looked at Ollie. "You would dress up like… me?" asked Samuel.

"Not like *those* clothes," replied Ollie, "I'd wear moccasins and war paint and carry a tomahawk or a bow and arrow and put feathers in my hair. I could have a big feather headdress!"

Samuel was shaking his head. "You would dress like a warrior and beg for food?" he asked. "I do not think that would be proper. You would make my people seem… dishonorable."

"But it'd be fun!" said Ollie. He made a pouty face.

"Um, we haven't decided on costumes yet, we're still making up our minds," I said. I didn't want Samuel to be upset.

"So how exactly did you dress, I mean, when you lived with the Wendat?" asked Sal. "Did you wear a little leather skirt thing around your waist?" He used his hands to show Samuel what he meant.

"When the weather was warm," said Samuel. "But we made clothing out of deerskins and furs for the winter.

We had long leggings and robes to keep us warm, and the women wore long skirts."

"Did you wear your hair in braids?" asked Ollie. "And have lots of feathers all around your head?"

Samuel shook his head. "One feather, or maybe two," he said. "Wendat women wore their hair in a braid, but most men shaved their hair except for their scalplock." He patted the top of his head. "Their scalplocks had longer hair."

"A Mohawk!" cried Ollie as his eyes lit up. "I can get a Mohawk for Halloween!"

"*Shut up*," I mouthed to Ollie.

"I was almost old enough to start wearing my hair like a proper Wendat man," said Samuel. "But when I came to the Mission, I had to cut my hair like a white child. Now I don't even look like a Wendat."

He looked sad as he said that, and I knew it was time to change the subject. "So what did you do today?" I asked.

"Let me show you!" said Samuel. He ducked back behind his shelf and came back with a roughly-carved piece of wood in his hands. "I am still just beginning. It is to be a hawk," he said. We could all see the basic shape of a bird.

"Wow! That's amazing!" said Sal, and we all agreed. "You are really good at that!"

Samuel smiled shyly. "I am only a beginner," he said. "But this is good practice for me!"

THE NEXT TIME WE visited Betty and Wally, Ollie sulked about the Halloween costume idea. "Why can't I be an Indian?" he asked.

"Our friend, the one we told you about? He thinks it's a bad idea to dress up in war paint and carry a tomahawk," said Sal.

"Well," said Betty, "I imagine he thinks dressing like an Indian for Halloween is disrespectful. You know a lot of sports teams that used Indian names are changing them now."

"But what's disrespectful about it?" asked Ollie. "I think it would be cool to wear war paint and carry a tomahawk!"

"Maybe your friend thinks it's a bad stereotype," said Wally.

"A bad what?" Sal asked.

"A stereotype. That's when we judge others by where they came from or what group they belong to, not on what we know about them as individual people. Most of us stereotype others without even thinking about it," said Betty.

"It's kind of like with your math class," said Wally. "Some people think girls aren't as good at math as boys. That's not based on fact, it's a stereotype."

"What if your math teacher decided you weren't as good at math as the boys in your class?" asked Betty. "Or, what if you both got jobs at the grocery store, and the manager told Sal he could work at the register and make change, but Orion had to stock shelves because she's a girl and girls can't make change. Do you see what I mean?"

"Your friend may think you're stereotyping all Native Americans as savage and uncivilized," continued Wally. "When I was growing up, movies always showed Indians attacking settlers and wagon trains and such. But many Indians were peaceful, and were very helpful to white people. Your friend's tribe probably just wanted to be allowed to live life their own way."

"Well," said Ollie, "I don't want to make Samuel mad at me. I guess I don't *have* to be an Indian for Halloween."

As we left the Howards' house, Ollie, who had been moping, brightened up. "Hey!" he said. "I've got an idea—let's take Samuel trick-or-treating with us!"

"Duh…he won't go out of the house!" I said. "There would be too many grownups around!"

"But wait," said Sal. "He'd be in a costume! Nobody would know who he is, so he wouldn't have to be afraid of anyone seeing him."

"Hmm," I said as I realized he was right. "It might

work. But he'd have to be totally covered up, 'cause he can't be seen in those awful old clothes of his."

"I know—he could be a ghost!" cried Ollie. "I mean, he *is* a ghost, but he could dress up as one! We could put a white sheet over him and cut holes for his eyes! Nobody would know what he looks like at all!"

"He won't eat the candy," said Sofi.

"That's OK," said Sal, "he can give it to us! You know, Ollie, sometimes you come up with great ideas!"

Ollie beamed, forgetting all about his disappointment over the Indian costume. "Where will we get a sheet for him?"

"We'll have to work on that," I said. "Let's all start thinking."

Chapter 14

A Whole Day with Samuel

Every year in October we get a four-day weekend when the schools hold parent-teacher conferences. This year, on the Thursday, we all did things with our own friends. I went to the mall with Mady and her mother, and bought a little twine bracelet with seashells on it. Ollie went with three friends to a pumpkin patch. Sal and Sofi spent the day with their mom, who had a day off work from the hospital.

On the Friday, Mrs. Martelli had to work a day shift, so Sal was going to baby-sit Sofi. He was to check in with my mom every hour. Mom said she would fix lunch for everyone and then take us all to a movie. That gave us the whole morning to visit with Samuel.

I had also decided I should try to draw a picture of

Samuel, and this would give me time to do it. I usually don't draw people—noses and ears are pretty hard—but I'm trying to practice and get better at it. I took my sketch pad and pencil, and we all clattered down the basement steps. Sal grabbed the marble bag and shook it.

"Samuel! Samuel, come out! It's safe!" he called. "My mom's gone all day, so we can talk as long as we want!"

A moment later Samuel appeared. Ollie and Sofi were jumping up and down.

"You are very happy about something," said Samuel.

"We have something exciting to tell you," said Sal. "We'd like to take you trick-or-treating with us. Remember, we told you about Halloween, when kids dress up in costumes and go door-to-door asking for candy? Well, we want you to go with us. You could dress in a costume that covers your head and clothes, so no one would know who you are. It'll be easy! You just follow along with us, and when someone answers the door, we say 'trick or treat,' and they give you candy and stuff."

Samuel was shaking his head. "Oh, no, there would be much too great a chance that I would be seen by grownups. I dare not go out of the house."

"You won't have to say anything, just do what we do," I said. "Nobody will hurt you—they'll just think you're another neighborhood kid. We'll dress you up as a ghost—that is, what people *think* a ghost looks like.

We'll put a white sheet over your head and cut out holes for your eyes so you can see. Plus, it'll be dark outside, and you'll be just another trick-or-treater. It'll be great!"

"It *would* be exciting to go outside!" said Samuel. "Let me think about it, please."

For once we didn't have to worry about the time, and didn't have to look over our shoulders or watch the clock while we talked to Samuel. I took my time with my drawing and tried to make a good picture of him. While I worked, we told him about our classes at school, the games we played, and places we'd visited. We also asked Samuel to tell us more about his life as a Wendat.

"Where did you live before you came to the Mission?" I asked.

"I was born near the great water, a great lake in the country called Ohio," said Samuel. "Before that, the Wendat lived far to the north. We lived in a village with some other families. We were at home on the water, and made canoes out of logs to travel the lake and the rivers. The land in Ohio was rich with deer and moose, and the waters were full of fish, and there were many kinds of birds, enough to feed everyone. In the forests we found nuts and berries, and we grew squash and beans and corn."

"Hold on!" said Sal. He ran up the stairs and returned a few moments later with the globe from his room. "Do you know what this is?"

Samuel had no idea, so Sal and I did our best to explain that it was a model of the earth where we lived. Sal pointed out the corner of Kansas where we were right then, then traced with his finger to Ohio. "Were you born near the Great Lakes? Look at the blue places—that's water. See, the gigantic blue parts are the oceans, and these big lakes must be where you used to live. They're in the north, where there's more trees and forests. That's where the deer would live. And the lakes would have all kinds of fish and birds."

Samuel was trying to get his head around the idea of the globe. "So the land—the place where we live, under the sun and moon and stars—it is round, like a ball of twine?"

"Yes," I said. "We have pictures of the earth from in space—you know, the sky—and we can see that it's round."

"Pictures from in the sky?" Samuel said. "The Wendat taught that long ago, the people used to live in the Upper World, like the sky. We used to sit around the fire and our grandfathers and grandmothers would tell us stories about how our people came down from the Upper World, but there were no pictures."

"So how did they get down from the Upper World?" asked Ollie.

"The story says a young woman fell out of the Upper World and landed in the water. She could not live in water, so she climbed onto the back of the great turtle. The other animals—the beaver, otter and toad—dived down into the water to get bits of soil that they put on the turtle's back to make an island. Then the woman had twins and soon there were people all over the island. We were known as the Island People."

"I like that story!" said Ollie.

"Me, too," said Sofi.

"But the white teachers told us our story was not true. They told us a different story about how men came to live on the land. They said we should forget the stories our grandparents told us."

"But you didn't, did you?" I asked.

"I will never forget," he said. He looked at the globe again. "And from where we are," he pointed to Kansas, "to here," he said as he put his finger on Lake Erie, "how far is that?"

"It's probably more than 500 miles," said Sal.

"How did you get from there to here?" I asked.

"We came in boats down the rivers, and we also walked a lot," said Samuel. "It was a long, hard journey and took many days. We were all tired and sad. My dog got lost, and many of the people got sick while we traveled, and died."

"I know how hard it is to move a long way from your friends," said Sal.

"I wish you could have gone in our car," said Sofi.

"Yeah," said Ollie, "those machines you've seen that go on their own without any horses to pull them."

"Did you have some friends who came to Kansas with you?" asked Sal.

"My good friend and kinsman, Thomas Walker, also made the trip. His father was my mother's brother and they lived in the same lodge with us. Thomas was just two moons older than I, and was like a brother to me. He also went to the Mission school, and we worked together in the woodshop, so I had someone to talk to about our life in Ohio. I know he was very sad when I died."

"What did the Wendat kids—I mean children—do in your village?" I asked.

"We helped our parents," said Samuel. "The boys learned to make canoes with the men, and we went hunting and fishing with them. I learned to use a bow and arrow and throw a spear. We helped prepare food, and the girls planted crops and helped the women make clothing from skins and furs."

"What kind of furs did you wear?" asked Ollie.

"Oh, beaver and fox," said Samuel. "The white people loved our furs, and sometimes we traded them for things they had, like knives and wool cloth."

"Did you have sports and games?" asked Sal. "What did you do for fun?"

"We played games with our friends, and ran races,

and climbed trees. We had contests of wrestling and strength. Thomas always beat me at the races, because he was taller and had long legs, but I could throw a spear the farthest! I missed my old home very much when we came to the west. There was no great water or vast forest here." He looked sad as he talked about his life before the journey. "And then, my parents died, and then Molly got sick…."

We all felt really sorry for Samuel, and crowded in close to him. "But now you have us for friends," said Sofi. "You don't have to be sad."

Sal looked at the clock, and told us it was time to leave for lunch. I'd gotten so involved in listening to Samuel tell about his life that I'd stopped drawing. I'd made a good start, though, and even though I was a little nervous about showing him, I turned the pad so he could see it.

"This is what I look like?" he asked.

"Well, you look better than this, but I'm not really finished," I said. "I haven't had much practice drawing people."

"You have skill with the pencil," he said. "I am honored to have you make my likeness." He liked it! I felt so proud, I decided to work extra hard at finishing it.

We told Samuel we would be back a little later. On the way to our house, Sal said, "You know what? We could bring Samuel upstairs for a while this afternoon, before we go to the movie. What do you think?"

"Oh, my gosh!" I exclaimed. "That's a great idea! We can show him your room, and the kitchen, and everything, and he can see what it's like to live like we do!"

Chapter 15

Samuel Takes a Chance

As we ate our macaroni and cheese, Mom said, "I hope you're not making a mess of the Martellis' house while Angie's at work. Maybe you should all stay here this afternoon instead of going back there."

"Oh, no, we haven't made a mess!" said Ollie.

"Honest, we haven't," said Sal. "We've spent most of the time in our playroom downstairs. We'll make sure everything's put away, OK?"

"Should I come over and check, so your mom won't have any unpleasant surprises when she gets home from work?" asked Mom.

"She won't even know we were there!" said Ollie.

"Well," Mom said to Sal, "I know you're a very responsible big brother, so I'll depend on you to take care of things."

We took Butterscotch with us back to the Martellis.' As we crossed the street, I said, "That was a close call. I was afraid my mom was going to come to your house and check on us."

We went back to the basement and jiggled the marbles. When Samuel appeared, we told him of the plan to take him upstairs. We could barely hide our excitement.

Samuel pulled back. "That is not a good idea. Are you certain your mother and father are not here? What if someone sees me?"

"But you've been upstairs before," said Sal. "You've been to my room and to Sofi's, too."

"Yes, when everyone was asleep, and I was sure I would not be seen," said Samuel. "I made my way to your rooms, because I was lonely. But I don't wish to go up there now."

"It'll be fine," Sal said. "Nobody else is here. We'll just go up for a little while. If somebody comes to the door or anything, Butterscotch will bark, and you can just come back downstairs. Don't worry."

"Please?" said Sofi. She took Samuel's hand, and he reluctantly came out of the little room.

"You've seen the playroom and the washer and dryer before," said Sal. "But there's lots of stuff upstairs that will knock your socks off!"

"Knock my socks off," mumbled Samuel as we crowded around him and headed for the stairs. We went upstairs to the kitchen first. Just turning on the light was a wonder to Samuel. "It is like the sun coming up inside the room," he said. "I have seen it happen downstairs, at night, from behind my shelf, but did not know how it was done."

"It's electricity," explained Sal. "Like lightning, in the sky? They make lightning and send it through wires to hook up to our houses, and we can turn it on and off!"

"You can do it, too!" said Ollie. "Here, just flip this switch!" Samuel turned the light off, then on, and off and on again. His face was full of wonder.

"But remember," I said, "you made the lights go out all by yourself, without the switch!"

Samuel looked down. "I will try not to do that again," he said. "But I must be very careful in case your mother or father comes to my room."

"Just stay behind the shelf unless we rattle the marbles," said Sal. "Now that we know about you, we'll never let you get lonely."

Samuel asked about every object he saw—the toaster, the refrigerator, the microwave. He recognized the sink for what it was, and, pointing to the faucet, asked, "Is this the water pump?"

We all laughed at that, but when he looked hurt, I said, "Don't feel bad—we're not laughing *at* you, we're laughing *with* you. It's just that it's a funny idea to us. Like to you, the things we have must seem funny."

"I laugh at Orion all the time," said Ollie, and Samuel relaxed. Sal showed him how the faucet worked, and how he could make the water change from cold to hot.

"You don't have to heat the water over a fire?" asked Samuel, amazed.

"No! And look at this!" exclaimed Ollie as he opened the refrigerator door. "Here's where we keep all the food that has to stay cold. And the freezer's on the bottom!" He opened the freezer and took out an ice cube, holding it out to Samuel.

"It's frozen water," said Sal. "Ice."

"I have seen frozen water. In Ohio the rivers and lakes would freeze in the winter," said Samuel, "but what are these small pieces for?"

"To make warm things cold," said Sofi. She took a plastic cup from the counter and filled it halfway with water, then put the ice cube in. "See? It'll make the water cold faster!"

Samuel gazed at all the things in the refrigerator, though he had no idea what most of them were. He touched a large white jug. "That is milk!"

"Yes!" I said. "And see, we keep fruit and vegetables in here, too, so they won't spoil."

Sal turned on a gas burner to demonstrate how the flame was controlled.

"And you don't need a fireplace? You never have to

worry that the fire will die and you'll have to start a new one," said Samuel, awe in his voice.

"And the microwave cooks even faster!" said Sal. He took a frozen hot dog out of the freezer and showed it to Samuel.

"That is…food?" said Samuel, touching the frozen hot dog uncertainly.

"It's meat," I explained. Sal put the hot dog on a plate, microwaved it for a few seconds and then took it out to show Samuel that it was not only thawed, but hot to the touch. Sal blew on it, then took a bite to demonstrate. He offered it to Samuel, but Samuel shook his head.

"Yeah, I forgot, you don't eat," said Sal.

The table and chairs in the kitchen caught Samuel's eye. "Someone worked many hours to sand and smooth and finish these," he said. "This is very fine workmanship."

"Uh, yeah," said Sal. "Let's go up to my room." Samuel was not really ready to leave the kitchen, but followed us toward the stairs. As we passed the hall storage closet, Sal suddenly stopped. "The vacuum cleaner!" he said. "Wait till you see this!" He pulled out the vacuum cleaner, plugged it in, and pushed it around on the floor.

"Get some cereal!" said Ollie. Sofi ran to the kitchen and came back with a box of Rice Krispies. Samuel looked closely at the cereal box and then peered inside.

"And what is this?" he asked.

Sal sprinkled a few Rice Krispies into Samuel's hand and said, "It's cereal. It's what we eat for breakfast. Here, put it on the floor." Samuel dropped the cereal onto the floor. Butterscotch sniffed at it before Sal vacuumed it up.

"You use that instead of a broom?" said Samuel, shaking his head. Sal put the attachment on the vacuum and held it on Butterscotch's back so that her fur stood up. Samuel put his hand under the attachment and laughed out loud.

"Come on!" said Ollie, leading the way to Sal's room as Sal put away the vacuum cleaner.

In the upstairs hall, Sal pointed out the bathroom. Samuel paused there for a moment, then said, "I think this is your outhouse."

We all giggled, and Sofi hopped in the tub. "This is where you take a bath," she explained.

"And there's a shower," said Sal. He pulled the curtain and turned on the water.

"It is like rain from the ceiling!" said Samuel as he looked in.

"And that's where you go to the bathroom," said Sal. He flushed the toilet so Samuel could see how it worked.

Even Samuel laughed then. "Oh, I see!" he exclaimed.

From there we went to Sal's room and then to Sofi's

room. He admired the posters on their walls, and their toys and books and clothes. He was impressed by the fact that they each had their own room.

"And our mom and dad have a room across the hall," said Sal.

"You are fortunate to have such a comfortable place to live," said Samuel.

Ollie shrugged and said, "We have all the same stuff at our house."

"Ollie!" I said. "Shut up! Samuel didn't get to live in a house like this."

Sal looked at the clock by Sofi's bed. "We'd better go," he said to me. "Your mom will wonder what we're up to."

Sofi went over to Samuel and gave him a hug. "I wish you could be my brother, and live up here with us," she said.

We all went back to the basement with Samuel. "Gosh, I wish you could stay. I hate to make you go back to wherever it is you go," said Sal.

"Do not trouble yourself over it," said Samuel. "Your world is marvelous, but I am content right here. I will go now and work on my woodcarving. But thank you for sharing these wonders with me today." He faded into the shelves. Out in the playroom, we checked to make sure everything was in order. "Did it make you feel sad for Samuel, not having all the stuff we have?" I asked. "I couldn't help feeling sorry that he had to work so hard, and live away from his family, and then, even worse, his parents and sister died!"

"Well," said Ollie, "*he* died too. That's the worst thing of all."

"But think about how hard his life was. I mean, he's right, we *are* lucky to be alive in the twenty-first century!"

Chapter 16

Getting Ready for Halloween

Later that evening, I went to my room to work on the drawing of Samuel. I had to erase a lot, but after a while I decided it was the best I could do. The next morning, I took the picture with me as I got ready to walk Butterscotch. I stopped over at the Martellis' house to show Sal and Sofi.

"It looks just like him!" said Sofi.

"You're a good artist," said Sal. "I could never do that."

He told me they'd had another close call as they told their mom and dad about their day.

"Yeah, I messed up a little," he said. "Mom asked me why there was a hot dog on the counter with the end bitten off. I didn't know what to say, so I told her Ollie did it."

"OMG," I said. "That's so funny!"

"It was a lie," said Sofi.

"I know, but it's the first thing I thought of! I should have put the hot dog down the garbage disposal. Promise you won't tell him? Please?"

I was laughing so hard I couldn't talk!

"I know I should've told the truth," said Sal. "I just hope she doesn't tell your mom."

HALLOWEEN WAS LESS THAN a week away, and lots of the houses in the neighborhood had cool fall decorations. A large spiderweb, complete with a black fuzzy spider, covered the front porch of one house, and another had fake gravestones with funny names like "I.M. Dead" and "Ima Goner" all over the front yard. Pumpkins and striped gourds were everywhere.

Ollie asked Mom and Dad if we could get a giant hot-air black cat like one he saw a few blocks over, but we had to settle for a scarecrow Mom made with old clothes and a floor mop. The Martellis placed pumpkins, gourds and Indian corn on top of a hay bale by their front door.

The closer it got to Halloween, the more excited we were about taking Samuel trick-or-treating. I had found an old sheet in the linen closet, and Ollie found an extra plastic treat bag for Samuel. To get Samuel out of the basement unseen, we made a plan: Sofi would have her parents help her with her costume in her room while Sal went to the basement to get Samuel ready. Then he'd sneak him quietly out the front door where Ollie and I would be waiting, and Sal would go back in and get Sofi.

A COUPLE OF NIGHTS before Halloween, I put Samuel's sheet over Ollie's head and marked the holes for his eyes with a black marker. "Uh-oh," I said, standing back. "I can see your feet. Samuel wears those old grungy boots—how will we cover them up?" I took the sheet off Ollie's head and cut the holes I had marked.

"He could wear my soccer shoes," said Ollie.

"Right!" I said. "Good thing you've got big feet. He'll still have to try them on to make sure they fit OK."

After school the next day we took the sheet and Ollie's soccer shoes to the Martellis' basement. We couldn't have him try on the shoes right then because Mr. Martelli was at home, but Sal said in a low voice, "Samuel, we're putting your Halloween costume here under the shelf. We'll come back soon and show you how to wear it."

Luckily we had Samuel try on the costume before Halloween, because once the sheet was over his head, we realized we had another problem. Not only his shoes, but his baggy, old-fashioned pants showed under the sheet.

"I know," said Sal. "You can wear some of my jeans. Hang on." He raced upstairs and grabbed an old pair of jeans from his dresser. When he got back downstairs, Samuel was trying on Ollie's shoes.

"They feel strange," he said.

"Do they hurt?" I asked.

"No, just—strange." Samuel did not know how to tie the shoes, so Ollie tied them, then we had Samuel walk around the basement a few minutes to get the feel of the shoes.

"Here, put these on, too," said Sal as he handed Samuel the jeans. Still under the sheet, Samuel slipped off his old pants and pulled on the jeans.

"Where are the rest of the buttons?" Samuel asked. "And what is this metal thing in the front?"

Sal rolled his eyes. "Oh, my gosh, the zipper," he said. "Turn around, you two." Sal pulled the sheet off of Samuel and, while Sofi and I turned our backs, he showed Samuel how to zip up the jeans.

"Hey, you look just like one of us!" said Sal, and we all agreed. The jeans were a little short on Samuel, but otherwise fit just fine.

"I'll bring you some socks, too, so the shoes won't feel so weird. This is going to be so cool!"

Chapter 17
The Big Night

───────────────────

Halloween came at last. Ollie and Sofi were in a frenzy, and Sal and I just tried to act like it was a normal day. We had a costume parade and class parties in the afternoon. Sal dressed as a robot, wearing a costume he made of cardboard boxes covered with aluminum foil. Sofi wore her Princess Elsa dress, and I went as a football player. Ollie went as a ghost—he had decided he liked Samuel's costume, and said that if there were two of them, nobody would know which was which.

We had an early dinner that night as Mom got ready for trick-or-treaters. I gulped down half of a ham sandwich, then took my plate to the counter. "Goodness, Orion," said Mom, "you seem even more excited by Halloween this year than ever before. I thought maybe you were getting too old for trick-or-treating."

"Mom! I'm only ten! Lots of kids bigger than me go out on Halloween!"

"Well, I'm glad to see you're still able to get into the spirit," said Dad. "Kids grow up too fast these days anyway."

I had to roll my eyes. I'd heard that line a bazillion times.

"I'm going to go get my costume on," I told my parents. "Dad, will you help me with the pads?"

I raced upstairs to get the football uniform I had borrowed from a high school boy we knew. Dad helped me attach the pads to my shoulders before I slipped on the red jersey, eye mask, and the helmet. Ollie came down a minute later wearing his sheet. We grabbed our treat bags and ran out the door.

When we rang the Martellis' doorbell, Sal answered, looking around him to make sure the coast was clear. He had on his robot costume, except for the head. He motioned us inside. "Mom, I'll be right back up—gotta grab something from downstairs!"

Mrs. Martelli called from up in Sofi's room, "Give us just a minute—we've almost got Sofi ready!" With that, Sal went down the stairs, and Ollie and I slipped back outside. Mrs. Martelli and Sofi came down the steps just as Sal and a white-sheeted ghost stepped from the basement.

"Heavens, Ollie, I wouldn't have known you!"

exclaimed Mrs. Martelli. "You look taller in that costume!"

Sal just grinned and said, "Gotta go now, Mom, everyone's waiting!" He put his robot head on and led the way out the door. Sofi grabbed the ghost's hand and followed Sal out into the night. They joined Ollie and me on the sidewalk.

"OK, Samuel, here's the heads up," I said. "You might see some costumes that look pretty scary, but don't let them bother you. They're all just kids like us."

It was a mild night, and most of the houses on the street had porchlights on to welcome the trick-or-treaters. We couldn't move too fast, because Sal couldn't see very well out of the robot head—he had to turn his entire head to look to either side. Samuel had time to gaze at the houses with their Halloween and fall decorations.

"What do you think?" I asked.

"So many houses! I did not know there would be this many!! Truly, this does not look at all like the place where I lived at the Mission," Samuel said.

"But don't you like being outside?" asked Ollie.

Samuel looked around. "It is quite wonderful," he said. "The night air, seeing stars and feeling the breeze…I didn't know how much I had missed it!"

"That's not the best part!" cried Ollie. "Wait till you see what we're gonna get!"

At the house next door to the Martellis,' we all went

up to the door and Sal rang the bell. "You don't have to say anything," he said to Samuel. "We'll say 'trick or treat' for you."

Mrs. Holmes answered the door, holding a bowl of chocolate bars. "Trick or treat!" we all sang out.

"Oh, my," said Mrs. Holmes, "what a group—and two ghosts!" She put a chocolate bar in each treat bag.

"Thank you!" everyone said, except for Samuel. As we walked back down the sidewalk, another group of trick-or-treaters was coming to the door. Samuel had taken the chocolate bar out of his treat bag and was looking at it closely. The other kids looked at him curiously. I heard one of them say, "Looks like he's never seen a Milky Way before!" They all laughed.

"Come on!" shouted Ollie. "We've gotta go!" Samuel looked up and hurried to join us.

At the next house we repeated the routine. This time Samuel joined us in the "trick or treat" and "thank you."

When we went across the street to the Howards' house, Wally answered the door. "Don't I know some of you?" he asked. "I'm sure I recognize those voices."

"Yeah, Wally, it's us," I said. "We're taking our friend with us this year." Wally let us choose our own candy. Samuel did as we did, and picked out a packet of M&Ms. "Thank you, happy Halloween!" we said as we ran down the sidewalk.

On we went, up and down the blocks, filling our bags

with Halloween loot. We met lots of other trick-or-treat-ers, mostly kids we knew from school. Samuel slowed as we approached a grisly-looking girl with fake blood on her neck and what looked like stitches all over her face. Sofi turned and took his hand, whispering, "It's not real, the blood's just painted on." Ollie dropped back beside them. They followed Sal and me as we passed the other group on the sidewalk.

"Cool makeup," I said. They all laughed, and we continued on our way. Samuel seemed really interested in the outdoor decorations—jack-o-lanterns, ghosts and bats hanging from trees, and a witch stuck on a tree as if she had collided with it in flight. He stared hard at a circle of grinning skulls in one front yard. Ollie and Sofi argued back and forth about which decorations were the best. "What do you like, Samuel?" asked Ollie.

"I have never seen such things in front of houses," he said. "They are quite unusual. But why are the ghosts—those white things that Ollie and I are dressed like—hanging from the trees?"

"Because ghosts are supposed to fly around, instead of walking," said Sal.

"The ghosts fly?" asked Samuel. "But why?"

Nobody knew the answer to that. "What about the costumes?" asked Ollie.

"They all look strange to me," Samuel replied. "Some make me want to laugh, but others are quite frightful."

"That's the whole idea," I said.

As we rounded the end of the block, I turned on the flashlight I had brought with me. Startled at the light, Samuel asked, "How did you do that?"

"Not so loud!" said Sal. "It's just a flashlight—it has batteries inside to make the bulb light up. I'll show you how it works when we're at home."

As we walked under a streetlight, Samuel sniffed the air. "I smell walnut trees," he said. "There!" He pointed to a scattering of black walnuts lying in the street. "Look, there must be half a bushel of them! Do you not gather the walnuts in the autumn to eat during the winter?"

I breathed in deeply. It was a familiar smell, but I'd never thought about actually eating the walnuts. I picked one up out of the street. "You mean you can eat these?" I asked.

"Yes, after the husk dries out, you scrape it off and crack the walnut shell. But it takes many walnuts for a winter's supply. It is a lot of work."

I was surprised at Samuel's ideas about the squash, pumpkins, and corn he saw on some of the porches. "Are they not afraid that someone will steal their food? Why do they leave it outside where anyone could take it?" he asked. "They should be storing these things for the winter."

"Oh, those are just for decoration. No one would steal them!" I said.

By this time, our bags were bulging and Sofi kept stepping on her dress. "I'm ready to go home," she said. Sal and I agreed.

Chapter 18
Looking for Molly

We really did plan to go home. Honest. But something—to this day I don't know what it was—made Sal and me look toward the Indian Mission. It was almost like we read each other's minds. I helped Sofi pick up the hem of her dress to keep from tripping and led the way one more block to the corner across from the Mission grounds. As we got near the big, brick buildings, Samuel stopped in his tracks. Nobody said a word for a few seconds.

"Samuel, do you know where we are?" asked Ollie.

"The Mission," he said as he looked around slowly. "I can never forget it. It was my home for two years."

Sofi took hold of Samuel's hand. All of a sudden, he broke free and ran into the street toward the Mission grounds.

"Watch out!" yelled Sal as headlights turned the corner and came toward us. "There comes a car!" I grabbed Sofi and Ollie by the hand as Sal lunged after Samuel and yanked at his sheet. The car slowed as Sal and Samuel stepped back toward the curb, then drove on.

"You have to watch out for cars!" yelled Sal, catching his breath.

"He doesn't know!" I yelled. "He's just not used to cars!"

We couldn't see Samuel's face, but he hung his head. "I am sorry," he said. "I did not mean to alarm you, but I was not thinking about the…car."

"Anyway, it wouldn't have hurt him if it had hit him," said Ollie. "You can't hurt a ghost, right?"

"Yeah, but it would've freaked the driver big time," said Sal. "OK, let's go now."

We crossed the street and stood under a tree in the yard of the biggest Mission building. A sign in the yard said it was the 'North Building.'

"Does it look the same?" asked Sal.

"The big buildings look the same," replied Samuel. "But everything else is much different. These houses were not here, and there were sheds and stables all around." He pointed at the building in front of us. "This is where I slept and ate. And over there," he said, pointing across the street, "that was where we had our lessons in the schoolroom. The woodshop is gone. Oh, and all these trees were not here." He waved his arms around at the grounds.

"I wish we could take you inside," said Sal. "You could show us where you and your friends slept."

"I do not wish to go back there," said Samuel. "I used to lie awake at night, thinking how much I missed my parents and friends, and wishing I could go back to the days when I ran races and wrestled with Thomas and hunted with Little Bear. And seeing it again is making me think of the day I tried to find Molly…."

"I guess we shouldn't have come here," I said. "I wasn't thinking about all the bad things that happened to you here."

"No, think nothing of it," said Samuel. "I just was not prepared for the memories it would bring back… it has been such a long, long time."

"Wait!" exclaimed Sal. "Where exactly was the cabin where Molly died?"

"Through there," said Samuel as he pointed up through the trees behind the long building. We all ran in that direction, staying in the shadows. Near the far edge of the grounds, Samuel stopped. "What is that big building?" he asked. "That was not here before."

"Oh, that's the high school," said Ollie.

"This is where you go to school?" asked Samuel.

We all laughed. "No, no!" I said. "We're not in high school yet!"

We went on past the front of the high school until Samuel stopped at a spot near the edge of the school driveway. "Here, I think," he said.

As we watched, Samuel walked in a circle, looking left and right. He put his hand on the ground in a couple of places, like he was feeling for something. As far as I could tell there was nothing there except grass and dirt. Finally, he said, "I believe my sister died near here, but her spirit is no longer here. I have not felt her presence since we arrived. I was hoping I would find her, at last…."

We all felt sad for Samuel right then, and nobody knew what to say. But then he looked at each of us and said, "Thank you for bringing me here. Now I know this is not her final resting place. I will just have to continue my quest to find her."

"We'd better get going," said Sal, putting his arm across Samuel's shoulder. "It's late and we're quite a ways from home."

Nobody said much as we headed back toward our own block. Most trick-or-treaters had gone home by now, and we needed to hurry. Just as we got to our corner, we met a group of middle school kids. They weren't really wearing costumes, just ragged-looking clothes. I recognized a boy named Brett and a girl named Amanda who had gone to Konza a few years ago. There were four of them in all, and they blocked our way on the sidewalk.

"Hey," said Brett, "it's the O'Briens, right? Who's with you?"

"Just our friends," I said, "and we're on our way home."

"You going out for the team?" the other boy asked me, and they all laughed.

"It's just a costume," I said. "Come on, Sal."

"Oh, Sally, is it?" asked Brett. "Sally who?"

"Let's go," said Sal.

"Hey, you're the new kid, right?" Brett said to Sal. He grabbed Sal's robot head and twisted it around so that Sal couldn't see. "How does that look now?" he asked, and they all laughed again. Sal twisted the head back so he could see, and glared at the bigger kids.

"And who do we have here?" asked Amanda, looking at Samuel.

"It's my cousin from New Jersey," said Sal. "He's just visiting for Halloween."

"Oh, don't they have Halloween in New Jersey?" asked the other girl. Samuel didn't answer.

"Can't you talk, New Jersey?" asked Brett.

"Come on, everybody, we've gotta get home!" I said, and grabbed Sofi's hand to lead her past the group of kids.

"Hold up, we want some candy," said one of the boys. He blocked the sidewalk, then took a step toward Ollie. "You can give us yours."

Chapter 19

Samuel Saves the Day

"No way!" said Ollie, and Sofi hugged her treat bag to her.

"You can get your own candy," I said. "Just go ask for it."

"It's easier to just take yours," said Brett, and he grabbed at Sal's treat bag. Sal jumped back out of his way.

"Let's go," Sal said again, and we all started backing up the sidewalk. Brett took a step toward us, like he was going to come after us. Just then, Samuel stepped in front of Brett.

"Only a coward would steal candy from smaller children," said Samuel, facing Brett down.

"Whoa! Who's a coward?" laughed the other boy.

"Maybe I'll just take yours, and they can all keep

theirs," Brett said to Samuel. Brett was a full head taller than Samuel, and heavier, too.

"You can have it," said Samuel, holding his treat bag out to one side, "if you can get it away from me."

"That'll be easy," said Brett, and he lunged at Samuel, grabbing for his arm, but Samuel twisted so fast that Brett missed. Samuel jumped aside and held out the bag in his other hand. Brett went for his arm again, and again Samuel twisted out of the way. I know I should have done something to help, but I just stood rooted to the spot. All I could think was, *please don't grab him! Please don't grab him!* But Samuel was having no trouble keeping away from Brett. The other boy and the girls started making fun of Brett.

"He's too fast for you," said Amanda. "Come on, let's leave these babies behind and go hang out at my house." This seemed to make Brett try even harder to get Samuel's candy.

"You think you're fast, New Jersey?" taunted Brett, as he shifted his weight from one foot to the other. He paused a few seconds, and then made one more dive at Samuel, like he was trying to tackle him. Samuel stood there waiting, and just as Brett was almost on top of him, he leaped backward, twirled in the air, and landed on his feet out of Brett's reach. Brett hit the ground with a thud.

The rest of us stood there with our mouths hanging

open. Before Brett could even get to his feet, Samuel turned and joined us, and we ran for all we were worth toward the Martellis' house. Nobody looked back until we got to the front walk. We stood there in a huddle, and saw the group of kids walking toward the other end of the block.

"Samuel, way to kick butt!" said Sal.

"You're the man!" said Ollie.

"A superhero!" said Sofi, giving him a hug.

"You really looked like a ghost flying through the air!" I said, rubbing the top of his head. "And you saved our candy for us!"

"In truth," said Samuel, "he could have had my candy. But it was wrong to try to steal it from us. I could not let him get away with that."

"But there were four of them!" said Sal. "Weren't you afraid? Those guys were a lot bigger than you!"

Samuel stood a little taller. "A Wendat must do the right and honorable thing, even if the odds are against him. I was taught to use my wits and my skills to overcome problems. But now my strength is nearly gone."

"Yeah, I'll bet," said Sal. "OK, you wait behind those bushes beside the house while we go in, and Sofi will get Mom to go upstairs and help her get her costume off. When they're out of sight, we'll signal to you. I'll meet you at the top of the basement steps and we'll go downstairs together."

We all went inside the Martellis' house to check out the situation. Mrs. Martelli came to meet us at the door.

"Wow, the neighbors here are very generous!" she exclaimed. "You've got a lot of candy!"

"It was fun!" cried Sofi, as she held her bag open to show her mother. Sal caught her eye and pointed up the stairs.

"Mommy, I tripped on my dress! Will you help me get it off?" asked Sofi.

"OK, let's just get you into your pajamas, and you can show us your candy after that," said Mrs. Martelli as she led Sofi upstairs.

"Where's Dad?" asked Sal.

"Oh, I think he's in the den watching the football game," his mother replied. "If any trick-or-treaters come, can you answer the door, please?"

"Sure," said Sal. Ollie and I said goodnight as Mrs. Martelli and Sofi disappeared up the stairs. Out on the porch, I waved Samuel up to the door. He slipped inside and met Sal at the top of the basement steps.

"You know what?" said Ollie as we crossed the street. "This was the neatest Halloween I've ever had! It's because of Samuel." For once, I agreed with my brother.

Chapter 20

A New Idea

The next day was a Friday, and I had a hard time getting out of bed because of all the excitement the night before. "It looks like you took in a pretty good haul this year," said my dad as he stopped in the kitchen on his way to the garage. "How long do you think your candy will last?"

"A long time!" said Ollie. "We're gonna get…"

I kicked him under the table.

"You're going to get what?" asked Mom.

"Wally and Betty said we could have some of their candy if they had any left over from last night," I said. "Sal and Sofi, too."

"Well, that's awfully nice of them, but I think you have enough," said Mom.

After school that day, we all met at the corner of our

street, where Sal divided Samuel's candy with the rest of us. "I think we pulled it off without a hitch!" he said proudly.

Saturday morning Sal telephoned to say his mom was going to the store and his dad was busy in the garage. Five minutes later Ollie and I were at the door, and we all headed to the basement to see if Samuel would come out. Sal rattled the marbles. In a moment Samuel appeared, still wearing Sal's jeans. He was holding the pocketknife and the wooden hawk, which was looking really fine.

"What did you think of Halloween?" we all blurted out at once.

Samuel took his time answering. "It was...strange and interesting," he replied. "I have thought about it very much. All the children were so excited, and the people at the houses were kind and friendly. But I cannot really understand the purpose of this...celebration."

"It's fun!" said Ollie.

"Yes, it was quite fun to go outside, and laugh and run. But many children's costumes and displays—like the gravestones we saw at some houses—reminded me of death. Death is not fun. Yet we asked for treats and enjoyed ourselves. This does not quite make sense to me."

"My teacher told us that Halloween used to be called

'Hallows' Eve'—the night before the day of All Hallows.' That's a celebration of the spirits of the dead, on November 1," said Sal. "So yeah, Halloween *is* kind of all about death. But it's fun because it's only make-believe."

"So we don't have to be afraid," said Sofi.

"And it was super-cool for us 'cause we know a real live ghost!" I added.

"You mean a real *dead* ghost," said Ollie.

"We didn't mean to make you feel sad about your parents and sister," I said. "Halloween's so much fun, I never thought about real people who died."

"We're sorry you didn't find Molly," added Ollie.

Samuel explained. "The Wendat always honored our ancestors who died. And we went to great lengths to show them respect. That is why I am so sad that I never saw Molly when she died. I never had a chance to do this for her! If she was not laid to rest on the Mission grounds, I don't know how I will ever find her."

"Gosh, I'm really sorry," said Sal. "I wish there were some way we could help you find out what happened to her." I felt a little guilty about him saying that, because we'd been so focused on Halloween, we'd forgotten to tell Samuel about the Indian cemetery.

No one else knew what to say, so Ollie broke the silence. "You did like the trick-or-treating, though, didn't you?"

Samuel brightened a bit. "I did like the trick-or-treating. It was so wonderful to be outside again. And seeing the squash and pumpkins and cornstalks reminded me of the crops my people used to grow—although we never cut faces into the pumpkins."

"That's called a jack-o-lantern," I said.

"Will you eat the pumpkin?" asked Samuel.

"Well…probably not. But we might bake the seeds to eat for snacks," said Sal.

"Why does everyone have so much food that they don't eat?" asked Samuel. "It seems very wasteful. You must have such good harvests every year that no one goes hungry."

"Oh…we get most of our food at the store," I said.

"The store?" asked Samuel.

"It's a big building where they have all kinds of food, and we just go there and buy it," said Ollie.

Samuel looked blank. Sofi changed the subject before we went any further with that. "Can I see your hawk?" she asked.

Samuel held out the wooden carving, which was really taking shape by now. "That is really good!" exclaimed Sal. "I can't believe you made that out of that block of wood!"

"It is not such good work," said Samuel. "My mother's father was the best wood-carver in our village. He could carve a bird in flight with its wings spread, and he had only a flint knife. I could never hope to be as fine a whittler as he was."

"I think it's beautiful!" said Sofi.

"I was learning to work with wood to do all kinds of things," said Samuel. "I helped put up frames for buildings, and I was training to do carpentry—making cabinets and dressers and other furniture. The whittling was just to pass the time."

Just then we heard the garage door close. "Sounds like my mom's home. We'd better go," said Sal.

"Do you want your pants and stockings back?" asked Samuel.

"Nah, you look good in them. You can keep them!" said Sal. Samuel grinned at us and disappeared into the shadows.

As Ollie and I walked toward our house, I said, "You know, we've still never told Samuel about the Indian cemetery. What if Molly is buried there? I think we should tell him."

"How can we find out if she's buried there?" asked Ollie.

"I'm not sure. Maybe we could ask Wally."

THE NEXT AFTERNOON, I saw Wally in his garden. It had frosted the night before, and he was cutting off tomato plants and picking the last of his squash. I went out to join him.

"Hello, young lady," said Wally. "Did you have a good Halloween this year? I liked your costumes."

"Oh, we had a great time! Wally, remember that Indian cemetery you told us about?" Wally nodded. "Is there a way to find out if someone is buried there?"

"Well, I expect so," said Wally. "There's probably a roster somewhere that tells who was buried there."

"What if we could go and see it? I mean, Sal and Ollie and Sofi and me? We could see who's buried there, couldn't we?" I asked.

"As far as I know, it's open to the public, so you could certainly go visit," said Wally. "It's not that far away, you know."

"I guess it's not. Yeah, maybe I could ask Grandma and Grandpa to take us there. Thanks, Wally, you always help me figure out what to do!"

Chapter 21

A Visit to the Graveyard

The next afternoon I walked home from school with Sal. I said, "Wally told me the Indian cemetery is open to the public, so that means we should be able to go see it. We need to get somebody to take us there."

"Would your mom or dad do it? I don't think my mom and dad even know where it is," said Sal.

"I was thinking of asking my grandma and grandpa. They live in Kansas City, Kansas, which is where the cemetery is. If I can get them to take us, do you want to go?"

"Sure," said Sal. "Let's say we need to see it for a school project. You did that mapmaking project, right? We could say you have to make a map of it."

"And we *are* studying history this year after all. I'll call Grandma when I get home."

I got the chance to call while Mom was fixing dinner. My grandparents grew up in Wyandotte County and lived there still.

"Hi, Grandma Libby," I said. "I have a favor to ask. Another kid and I are working on a history project at school, and we want to visit the Indian graveyard. Would you and Grandpa take us there? You know where it is, don't you?"

"Yes, I know," said Grandma. I heard her say something to Grandpa Louie, then she said, "We could take you on Saturday afternoon. How does that work?"

"Thanks, Grandma!" I nearly shouted. This was going to be easier than I thought. I called Sal to invite him and Sofi to meet us at our house for the trip.

So, on Saturday afternoon, Sofi and Sal came over to wait for Grandma Libby and Grandpa Louie. They arrived in their old blue van, which had plenty of room for all of us. I introduced Sal and Sofi to them, and everybody got buckled in.

"Do you know where the Indian graveyard is?" asked Sal.

"Oh, sure," said Grandpa Louie. "I grew up not far from there. I've walked by it a hundred times, but only been up in it a few times. What are you doing for your school project?"

"It's for fifth grade history," I said. "Sal's class is doing a unit on Native Americans, and my class is doing map-

making. Wally Howard told us about the Indian graveyard, and we thought it would be a good place to visit.
I'll try to make a map of it."

"And I wanted to see it, too!" said Ollie. "Grandma,
will you take pictures of us there?"

"I think we could handle that," she said.

It took about twenty minutes to cross the bridge over
the Kansas River and park near the cemetery entrance.
At the front there was a big stone sign that said 'Huron
Indian Cemetery,' and there were plaques telling about
Wyandot history and the animals that were important
to them. I noticed that there were different kinds of tur-
tles. Grandpa Louie stopped to read the plaques while
the rest of us went up to the cemetery grounds.

The graveyard itself was really cool. It was on the top
of a flat-topped hill, and we could look down on the city
buildings and streets. There were lots of big, old trees
all around, and some still had a few pretty leaves hanging on. An old stone wall went all around it. We saw a
few big headstones, and lots of small, plain stones on the
ground. They looked dark and super ancient.

I walked around the graveyard with a pad and pencil,
sketching out the locations of gravestones and trees. Sal
went from gravestone to gravestone, writing down the
names he found on them in a notebook. Ollie and Sofi
ran around through the grass, until Grandma Libby
reminded them where they were.

"This is the resting place for people who have died," she explained. "We have to show them respect." Ollie and Sofi stopped running, and instead tiptoed around looking at the old headstones. Grandma Libby snapped a few photos of Ollie and Sofi beside some of the stones, and even let Ollie take a selfie.

There weren't as many headstones as I expected. Lots of them were hard to read because the letters were worn away. We found some that were more than 100 years old, and I even saw a few dates from the 1700s! We looked for stones with dates from the 1840s, but were disappointed to find no headstone for Molly Grayhawk. Then we found a marker that said there were probably 400 people buried there who couldn't be identified. After a while we started to get chilly, so Grandma and Grandpa took us home.

The next Saturday night, we built a fire in the fireplace for the first time that fall. Mom and Dad invited the Martellis to join us for burgers that my dad grilled on the back porch. We sat in front of the fire while the grownups talked in the kitchen.

"You know, we have to tell Samuel soon about the Indian cemetery. Ever since Halloween, he seems to be thinking about Molly all the time," I said.

"I know," said Sal, "but what if she's in one of those graves that can't be identified?"

"Well, if we could just take him there, maybe he could

feel her spirit or something—whatever ghosts can do," said Ollie.

"But how can we get him there? We can't take him with my grandparents, because we'd have to explain who he is!" I said.

"Do you think we could tell Wally and Betty about him?" asked Sal. "They wouldn't ask as many questions as our parents—you know, like, whose class is he in, and where does he live."

"I don't know…maybe," I said.

"But it might be our only choice," said Sal. "We might just have to trust them."

We had noticed a change in Samuel since Halloween. He was quieter and more thoughtful. We had a long visit with him a week before Thanksgiving.

"We can tell you've seemed sort of sad lately," I said. "Is anything wrong? Are you mad at us?"

"No," said Samual, "I only keep thinking about Molly and how I must find her to honor her spirit. Ever since the trick-or-treating I have been reminded to do my duty as her brother. But I am not mad at you. You, too, are my brothers and sisters."

Ollie and Sofi looked at each other with huge grins.

"What exactly will you do to honor Molly when you find her?" I asked.

"The Wendat were very sad when someone died,"

Samuel replied. "We brought gifts to bury with them, to show our love and respect."

"What kind of gifts?" asked Ollie.

"Furs, shells, beads, cooking pots, things like that," said Samuel. "I have nothing to bring her, so all I can do is tell her how much she meant to me."

"We really want to help you find Molly," said Sal. "I just know we can think of something if we try."

"I know that and I am grateful. I will try not to be sad."

"We're getting ready for another big holiday," said Sal. "It's called Thanksgiving, and it's when we give thanks for all the blessings we have in our lives. We have a huge meal with lots of food, and we don't have to go to school."

"We also celebrated with feasts," said Samuel. "I loved the feast of the Green Corn—we ate *so* much! And we had feasts when someone died." He looked sad again as he said this.

"I wish you could come to our Thanksgiving dinner," said Sofi. She was sitting next to Samuel, and put her arms around his neck.

"But our parents will be there," said Sal. "And anyway, you wouldn't eat the food."

"You can tell me about it after. I will have plenty of time to whittle on my hawk," said Samuel.

Chapter 22

Hope for Samuel

Thanksgiving week has always been one of my favorite times of year—no school, lots of food, company, and the holiday atmosphere. Grandma Libby and Grandpa Louie would be coming for dinner. The Howards' daughter and grandkids from St. Louis would be arriving on Wednesday. And the Martellis would be spending their first Thanksgiving in Kansas with just the four of them, because the airfare to New Jersey and back was more than they could spend this year.

The day before Thanksgiving, Ollie and I helped Mom tidy up the house for the next day. In the afternoon we went to see Sal and Sofi, who were disappointed at not seeing their grandparents for Thanksgiving.

"Hey, it'll be fun anyway," I told Sal. "It's a long break

from school, and you can come to our house as much as you want."

"I know. I was just hoping to go back to New Jersey and see my friends again," Sal said. "But then I would miss seeing Samuel, and besides, I couldn't really tell my friends about him."

Mrs. Martelli looked in from the kitchen. "I have to run to the store for some chicken broth," she said. "I'll leave Sofi here with you, OK?"

"Sure," said Sal.

"This is our chance to tell Samuel about the cemetery!" I said as soon as Mrs. Martelli was out the door.

"Right," said Ollie. "He seems so sad lately. We have to help him find Molly!"

"I know," said Sal. "He's been trying to find her for like 100 years! He's probably starting to lose hope."

Sal ran upstairs to get his notebook and the map I had made of the cemetery. We went to the basement and Sofi rattled the marble bag. It was only a moment before Samuel appeared, still wearing Sal's jeans and socks. We all sat down in a circle. "My mom will be back soon, but we've got something to tell you," Sal began. "Why don't you tell him, Orion?"

I took a deep breath. "Well, our neighbors have been helping us find out about the Wyandot people, and they told us that there's an Indian cemetery not far from here and…"

"An Indian cemetery?" Samuel interrupted, which was very unusual for him. "You mean…?"

"A graveyard. We found out that Indians who lived at the Mission were buried there when they died," I went on. "The problem is, we don't know whether Molly is there or not. We went there one day—all of us—and looked at all the headstones, but we didn't find one with her name on it."

"And we know that lots of people were buried there with no headstones," said Sal. "And some headstones have been lost and destroyed over the years. We looked at all of them."

"Anyway," I continued, "that doesn't mean that Molly isn't buried there, it just means there's no gravestone for her. So…we were thinking, maybe if *you* went to the cemetery, you would be able to tell if she's there. You know, like you tried at the Mission?"

"Maybe you can tell if her spirit is there," finished Sal.

Samuel was very quiet. "You actually saw this place?" When everyone nodded, he went on, "It is my greatest desire to find my sister Molly, just to know where she is laid to rest. I would be able to honor her, and her spirit would rejoice knowing I am with her. Please, tell me more about the Indian cemetery!"

"Well, the sign at the front calls it the 'Huron Cemetery,' but from what our friend Wally told us, it's the place where the Wyandots who came here from Ohio were buried," I said.

"The Huron?" said Samuel. "That is the name given the Wendat by the French."

"There's a sign that says maybe hundreds of people are buried there!" said Ollie.

"And we looked all around it, and I wrote down some of the names I found on gravestones," said Sal. He checked his notebook. "James Bigtree, Tall Charles, lots of Zanes. And some chiefs—Francis Hicks and James Washington. Oh, and listen to this—there was a head-stone for 'Ron-Ton-Dee.'"

"Ron-Ton-Dee!" exclaimed Samuel. "I knew that man! He was a chief of our people! He had the white-man name of Warpole."

"Yeah, that was on the headstone, too," said Sal. "Oh, and there were lots of Armstrongs and Walkers."

Samuel looked at Sal. "I wonder if one was for my kinsman Thomas," he said.

"I don't remember a Thomas," said Sal.

"I would like to think Thomas grew up and had a good life," said Samuel.

"Here's a map I drew of the cemetery," I said, show-ing it to Samuel. "Most of the graves are here," I pointed out, "but they're scattered all over the grounds. I marked where the entrance is, and the big trees, and where some of the people are buried. These rectangles are gravestones. And here's the sign that tells about all the unknown people who are buried."

"Maybe Molly is buried in one of those 'unknown' graves," said Ollie. "Do you want to go and see?"

Samuel was thoughtful. "How can we can do this?"

"It won't be easy," said Sal. "It's too far to walk there, and we're too young to drive, so we have to get someone to take us. And we also have to explain *you*."

"But that won't be hard!" said Ollie. "Look at him— he looks just like any other kid in Sal's jeans and socks. We could find a better shirt for him, and nobody would know he's a ghost at all!"

"Ollie, you're brilliant!" said Sal. He dashed up the stairs and came back a moment later with a Mets sweat-shirt. "Here, put this on!"

Samuel looked at the shirt and said, "Mets?"

"Yeah, it's a baseball team, like Ollie's Royals," said Sal. Samuel slipped the sweatshirt on over his own ragged shirt. After I straightened his collar and brushed his hair off his face, he could pass for a twenty-first century boy sitting with his friends. He looked down at himself, then up at us, and broke into a huge smile. "Please tell me you will be able to take me to find Molly!"

"We'll do our very best," said Sal. "We better go now— we'll keep you posted."

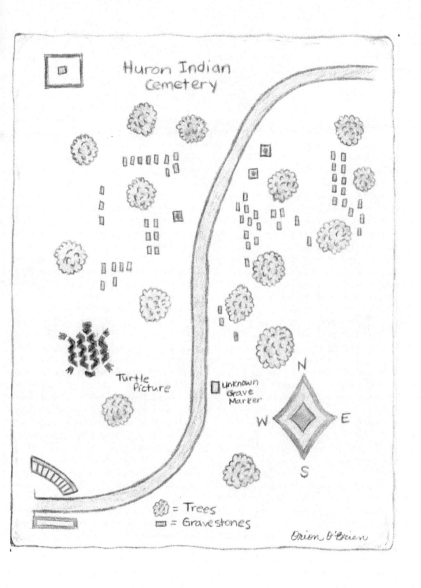

Huron Indian
Cemetery

Turtle
Picture

Unknown
Grave
Marker

N
W   E
S

= Trees
= Gravestones

Orion O'Brien

Chapter 23

A Thanksgiving Plea

Thanksgiving Day started out with a frosty morning, with the leaves in the yard twinkling like diamonds. It was cold, but the sun was bright. Our house smelled of roasting turkey, spices, and cinnamon. Ollie and I watched TV in the family room, but popped in to the kitchen every so often to check on the food. Finally Mom put a white tablecloth on the dining room table and set out plates and silverware. She told me and Ollie to set the table for seven.

Grandma Libby and Grandpa Louie arrived with my great-grandma, Grandpa Louie's mother. We call her Granny Bets, and she's like 100 years old. They brought apple pie, baked sweet potatoes, and fresh homemade hot rolls, which they added to the dishes already on the table—turkey, dressing, green beans with bacon, and cranberry sauce. After we all sat down, each of us told what we were thankful for. I really wanted to say I was thankful for meeting Samuel, but that would just bring a lot of questions. Instead, I said I was thankful for my new friends and neighbors. Ollie said he was thankful for his family—even his sister—and his special friends. I knew exactly who he meant.

The Martellis celebrated with just the four of them for the first time ever, but it was still a special day. Sal and Sofi made a centerpiece for their table by sticking colored feathers in a pine cone to look like a turkey. After the table was all set, they Facetimed their grandparents in New Jersey. Their grandparents surprised them with the news that they were invited back to New Jersey for Christmas, so the whole family would be together then.

"We're starting a brand new tradition," said Mr. Martelli. "We're the first Martellis to have Thanksgiving in Kansas—just like the Pilgrims were the first Englishmen to celebrate in America!"

Sal thought to himself, "Yeah, and just like the Pilgrims, we know a real Indian."

As their parents set dish after dish on the table, Sofi whispered to Sal, "I wish we could bring Samuel upstairs to eat with us."

"He doesn't eat!" whispered Sal.

"I know, but I just want him to be here with us," she said.

WE HAD AGREED TO go visit Wally and Betty after our Thanksgiving dinner, so Ollie and I ran across the street to get Sal and Sofi. Out on the sidewalk, I said, "It's now or never. We have to ask Wally if he'll take us to the cemetery."

"What are we gonna tell him?" asked Sal. "We can't tell the truth!"

"But we promised Samuel! And he's dying to find Molly!" I said.

"He's already dead," said Ollie.

"*Please*," I said, glaring at him. He can be *such* a pain. "Really, we promised, and we can't let him down! This is our only chance!"

So, we ran to the Howards' front door. Betty let us in and took us to the family room, where Wally was sitting in his recliner. Their daughter Jennifer, her husband and two little kids were getting ready to go visit friends.

"Happy Thanksgiving!" we shouted.

Wally invited us to sit down and then said, "Sal, remember you asked me if anything strange ever happened in your house? I told you there had been a family years ago who only lived there a short time. Well, I asked

Jenny if she remembered anything about them. She was in school with their two little boys."

Jennifer was busy trying to get her four-year-old to put on his coat, but said, "Yes, I remember them. They had two boys a little younger than me, and I didn't know them very well, but a story went around school that the littler one told someone he talked to an Indian boy in the basement. I guess their mom actually heard him talking to someone down there, and was pretty upset about it. He was so little, he probably just had an imaginary friend. Anyway, before we knew it they'd moved out."

"Sounds more like an over-anxious mother than anything strange in the house," said Betty.

"Have you seen something strange since you moved in?" Jennifer asked Sal.

Ollie's head jerked up, but I gave him a 'keep-quiet' look.

"Oh…not really…there were a few things, but I figured out the explanation for them," said Sal.

"That's good," said Jennifer. "Nobody else ever had any problems there, as far as I know." She herded her kids out the door and said goodbye.

I think we were all a little spooked by what Jennifer had told us, and nobody said anything for a minute or two. Finally, Sal said, "We're here to ask a favor. Remember our friend we told you about, whose ancestors are Wyandot Indians? And you told us about an Indian cemetery not far away." Wally nodded. "Well, we need to find a way to take our friend to visit the cemetery."

"But we can't ask our parents to take us," I continued, "because they don't actually know about him."

Wally raised his eyebrows. "They don't?"

"Is there some problem with him?" asked Betty.

"Well...Samuel—that's his name—isn't really like other kids," I explained. "He...he doesn't really have a family who can help him, and he wants to find out if his...relatives...might be buried in the Indian cemetery."

"I think there's something you're not telling us about Samuel," said Betty. "What is it?"

I looked at Sal and swallowed. I thought to myself, *We're gonna have to tell....* My mind raced, wondering what to say without sounding insane. "Ummm..." I started.

"Now this is just a guess," said Wally, "but didn't you tell us his family is dead? Orion...Sal...is Samuel *homeless*?"

Sal and I looked at each other and slowly nodded. "Well...yeah, that's it," said Sal. "So, we can't tell our parents about him, because he doesn't want any grownups to know. He's afraid someone will come and take him away."

"And he's very shy—he would never ask you to help him, but we thought since you know about the things that happened to the Wyandots, you might help us get Samuel to the cemetery," I said hopefully.

Wally and Betty said nothing for a few seconds. Finally, Betty said, "You've known Samuel for some time now, haven't you? A homeless child is a serious matter, especially now that cold weather is here. Have you tried to get him to ask for help finding shelter and food? I'm surprised you haven't told your parents."

"He doesn't—" began Ollie.

"He's a little older," I said, and shot Ollie another warning look. "He's not going hungry or anything."

"And we've talked to him about getting some help," said Sal. "But…*this* is what he's asked us to do. Please? It would mean so much to him!"

"And we really love him," added Sofi.

"I can tell you care about him a great deal," said Wally. "Don't you want to do what's best for him?"

Sal squirmed. "Yeah, but…the thing is, he's trying to find a way to…fix his situation…on his own, and he'd be really upset if he knew we're telling you about him."

"And," said Ollie, "you've already seen him. He went trick-or-treating with us."

Betty and Wally looked surprised at that. "What exactly do you want us to do?" asked Betty.

"How about this?" I said. "If you'll take us—and

Samuel—to the cemetery, then afterward we'll do whatever we have to do to help him find a home." I looked at the others. "Is that OK with everybody?"

It was agreed that on Saturday, after Jennifer and her family left for St. Louis, Betty and Wally would take us all to the Indian cemetery. As we walked down the Howards' front walk, Ollie said, "I can't believe you told them that we'd find him a place to live!"

"What else was I supposed to say?" I shot back. "I had to get them to say 'yes!' Besides, I never said exactly *what* we'd do, and if he does find Molly, it could change everything!"

"If he finds her," said Sal, "he needs something to give her. Remember, he told us they give gifts to the dead people when they bury them."

"Oh, yeah," I answered. "He said shells, furs, beads…"

"Marbles!" said Sofi.

"Yes!!" cried Ollie. "He loves the marbles! He thought they were beads!"

"Come on," said Sal, and we all raced back across the street to the Martellis' house. Ollie, Sofi and I went upstairs to Sal's room, while he went to the basement to get his marble bag. He came upstairs a minute later.

"I had to be real careful not to rattle them," he said. "I didn't want Samuel to hear them and think it was safe to come out."

Sal poured the marbles out on his bed and said, "OK, everybody pick one." He had a lot of pretty ones, so I chose an orange, gray and white agate. Sal picked a shiny blue one, Sofi picked a green and gold cat's eye, and Ollie picked a red and yellow one. We agreed to give them to Samuel right before we left for the cemetery.

"Let's hope they bring good luck," said Sal.

While we were picking out the marbles, Mrs. Martelli stuck her head inside Sal's door. "You kids have been getting kind of messy in the basement," she said. "I saw what looked like wood chips on the floor downstairs."

Oops! I was totally not ready for this! I hope I didn't look too alarmed as I looked at Sal. Hard as it is to believe, my brother came through with an answer. "Sorry!" said Ollie. "I got wood chips in my shoes at the park. I'll clean it all up!"

"I'll help!" I said, and we all scrambled back to the basement to sweep up the chips.

"Good call, Ollie," said Sal as he grabbed the broom and dustpan.

"Yeah," I agreed. "Maybe you're not so dumb after all."

Chapter 24

A Trip for Samuel

Friday after Thanksgiving, we started begging Mom to let us go get a Christmas tree when Dad got home. She sent us upstairs to clean our rooms, but promised we could look for a tree very soon. Ollie put away toys for about five minutes, then came over to my room and picked up the Amazon Fire. We spent about an hour looking for photos of Native Americans. Ollie was still impressed by the ones with war paint and feather head-dresses.

"Are you nervous about tomorrow?" asked Ollie.

"Of course!" I said. "This has just got to work, because I don't have any other ideas!"

Sal and Sofi spent the day at home with their mom, who had the day off work. They helped make biscotti, Italian cookies they always made at holiday time. Late in the afternoon, when Mrs. Martelli was busy in the kitchen, they went down to see Samuel for a few minutes. (I couldn't believe they took such a chance with their mom home, but Sal said he just couldn't resist.) Samuel showed them the wooden hawk he was carving. By this time they could clearly make out the feathers, eyes, and beak.

"It's awesome!" said Sofi.

Sal agreed, but his main concern was for the next day's plans. "Are you ready?" he asked Samuel.

"Do not forget how long I have waited," said Samuel. "I am more than ready."

"What if you don't find Molly?" asked Sal.

"Then I must keep trying to find her," said Samuel. "But I am very hopeful."

"We have to go now," said Sal. "We'll all see you tomorrow!"

SATURDAY WAS GRAY AND overcast, and snowflakes flurried off and on. Mrs. Martelli had to work a shift at the hospital, so Sal and Sofi were with their dad all day. They told him they were invited to go see some local Christmas lights with the Howards that afternoon. Mr. Martelli said we could all come back for a spaghetti dinner afterward. My mom and dad went Christmas shopping, so Ollie and I huddled in Sal's room to figure out how to get Samuel from their house to the Howards.'

"Maybe we should blindfold him so he won't freak out over the cars and everything," suggested Ollie.

"No!" said Sal. "That would be mean!"

"Right, and how would we explain that to Betty and Wally? Get real. We'll just have to tell him not to worry about anything he sees," I said. "He's never ridden in a car, and he's nervous around grownups."

"It's cold out today!" said Sofi. "He should have a coat."

"Hmm, he won't get cold, but he might look funny without one, so I'll grab a hoodie for him," said Sal. "Here's what we'll do. I'll keep my dad in the kitchen until you guys get out of the house with Samuel. You all head over to Wally's and I'll catch up with you."

We were to meet the Howards' at 2:45, so at 2:30 we all went to the basement. Mr. Martelli was in the family room reading. Sal turned on the MP3 player and cranked up the volume as Sofi and Ollie jumped around and sang along in the playroom. Sal and I went into the little room and rattled the marbles. "Samuel!" we whispered. "It's time to get ready to go! Come out as quiet as you can!"

Samuel appeared almost immediately. Sal handed him the hoodie and showed him how to pull the hood up over his head. "It's cold out today, and you've got to look like you're dressed right," I said. We hadn't thought to bring mittens or gloves, but showed him where to tuck his hands in the front of the hoodie.

"Now remember, we're going to be with grownups," I said. "Their names are Wally and Betty and they're real old. We went to their house on Halloween. We'll be going in their car. I know it'll be scary for you, but just don't panic, and we'll take care of everything."

"You're going to their house with Orion and Ollie and Sofi, while I keep my dad out of the way," said Sal. "Are you ready?"

Samuel nodded. "I have to be brave so I can find Molly," he said.

"I know you're brave," said Sofi, smiling up at him.

"Oh, and one more thing," Sal said as Sofi turned off the music. He pressed the marbles we had picked out into Samuel's hand. "Just in case you find Molly," he went on, "here's a marble from each of us for you to give to her."

"And you can take this to her, too," I said, taking the shell bracelet off my wrist and handing it to him. Samuel looked down for a minute, and I thought he might be about to cry, but then he looked up and put the marbles and bracelet in his pocket.

"Thank you," he said quietly. "If Molly is there, these gifts will show honor to her."

It was time to go, so Sofi and Ollie ran upstairs to get

their coats. Sal went next, and I waited with Samuel at the bottom of the steps. I heard Sal talking to Mr. Martelli.

"Dad, we're leaving to meet Betty and Wally. I thought it might be nice to take them some biscotti," said Sal. "Would that be OK?"

"That's a good idea," said Mr. Martelli. As he and Sal went into the kitchen, Ollie motioned to me from the top of the basement steps. Samuel and I hustled upstairs where I got into my coat as fast as I could while Samuel stood near the front door. Then we all charged out the door at once. We ran as fast as we could to the Howards' house and rang the bell. As soon as Betty opened the door, Sal came running up the steps behind us with a bag of Italian cookies in his hand. We practically fell into the house. "We made it!" cried Sal.

Then we remembered our manners, and I introduced Samuel to Betty and Wally. Samuel looked nervous, but said, "I am very pleased to meet you." Betty was looking at him really close, and I was glad he was wearing Sal's clothes. Except for his hair being sort of long, he could have been any neighborhood kid.

Sal gave Betty the biscotti. She thanked him, and Wally said, "I think we should just get going. It'll get dark pretty early, and it's blustery and cold—it might even snow."

So, we went to the garage and piled into the Howards'

ancient station wagon. It was the kind with a third seat that faced out the rear window. Ollie and Sofi sat there, and Sal and I put Samuel between us in the seat behind Wally and Betty. Sal buckled Samuel's seat belt.

Wally opened the garage door with the automatic opener and started the car. Sal and I were both praying that Samuel would stay calm and not freak out. I leaned close to him, and Sal put his hand on Samuel's shoulder reassuringly.

"Samuel, I understand this is your first trip to the cemetery," said Betty.

"Yes, ma'am," said Samuel. I thought to myself, it's his first trip ever in a *car*.

"Do you go to school with Sal and Orion?" asked Wally.

"No, sir," said Samuel.

"Not a big talker, are you?" Wally said.

"He's got a lot on his mind," I said. "And like we told you, he's really shy."

"There's nothing wrong with being shy," said Betty. After that, she and Wally talked quietly to each other and didn't ask Samuel any more questions.

Samuel leaned closer to Sal. "Who is that I hear talking?" he asked.

"You mean Betty and...? Oh, the radio!" he whispered. "Kind of like the television, but no picture—only sound."

Samuel quietly looked out the windows for the rest of the trip. Ollie and Sofi chattered in the rear and giggled about riding backwards.

We arrived at the cemetery and parked by the entrance. We didn't see anyone else there. Everyone got out and started up the hill to where the graves were. Samuel stopped after a few steps. "Please," he said, "may I go alone?"

Sal patted Samuel on the back and said, "Sure." And we all watched as Samuel slowly walked up the path to the top of the hill.

Chapter 25

Molly's Spirit

Betty and Wally went to read the plaques about Wyandot history while Ollie and Sofi ran back and forth on the sidewalk below the cemetery to keep warm. Sal and I decided to walk around the outside of the cemetery. "We'll meet you back here," we told Wally.

We caught glimpses of Samuel as he reached the hilltop and looked around in wonder. He walked around the grounds, examining the headstones. Several times he stood and cocked his head, like he was listening for something, then continued his search of the graveyard.

When Sal and I got back to the entrance, Sofi and Ollie ran to meet us and we joined Wally and Betty. We all started up the path to the burial ground. When we reached the hilltop, Samuel was nowhere in sight. Then, when the wind died for a moment, we heard a voice.

"There he is!" whispered Sofi, pointing. And sure enough, Samuel sat cross-legged under an enormous tree, eyes closed, softly chanting in a language we had never heard. Even though we didn't understand the words, we knew it was really sad. Then Samuel fell silent, but remained seated with closed eyes.

After a moment, without a word, all four of us ran to his side and fell to our knees, hugging him as tightly as we dared.

"Did you find her? Is she here?" whispered Ollie.

Samuel opened his eyes and looked at each of us. "I feel the spirit of my sister here, under this tree. Her grave is not marked by a stone, but I can feel her reaching out to me." He pointed to the ground in front of him, where we could see he'd dug into the dry grass with a stick. "I buried the marbles and shells for her here. I have honored my sister."

Wally and Betty had followed us to where we sat. No one said anything, but I'm sure they could tell something pretty important had just gone down. After a few minutes, Betty reached down, took Sofi's hand, and helped her to her feet. "I think we'd better go now, dear," she said.

No one spoke on the way back to the car. After we were buckled in, Wally drove through the Country Club Plaza to see the lights. They looked amazing, thousands of them shining through the misty air. Samuel probably didn't have a clue about Christmas lights, but I didn't dare ask him what he thought. He was really quiet and seemed to be thinking a lot. It was almost dark by then, and we needed to get home for dinner.

Back at the Howards,' we all thanked Betty and Wally, and all of us except Samuel gave them each a hug. (I was relieved that Betty and Wally didn't try to hug or touch him—who knows what they would have thought?) Samuel said, "I am very grateful to you for what you have done for me. I will not forget your kindness." Then we said our goodbyes and left for the Martellis.' Ollie and Sofi went in the house first and cornered Mr. Martelli in the kitchen, telling him about the Plaza lights. Sal and I hurried Samuel inside and down the basement steps. "We'll see you soon!" said Sal as Samuel made for the corner of the little room.

I gave his hand a squeeze. "I'm so glad you found her!" I said. Samuel was already almost invisible as I let go of his hand and turned to follow Sal upstairs.

Chapter 26

Will Samuel Go?

I woke up Sunday morning with a sick feeling in my stomach. I went to Ollie's room and woke him up. "I'm going crazy, wondering what will happen now with Samuel," I said.

"Me, too," he said. "Do you think we'll get to see him today?"

"I hope so!"

"Well, remember, we get to go look for a Christmas tree today!" said Ollie.

"Yeah, maybe that'll help us keep from worrying all day about Samuel," I said.

SAL TOLD M E LATER he'd had a hard time getting out of bed Sunday morning. He went across the hall to Sofi's room, and whispered, "I dreamed that Samuel was in my room last night."

"I did, too," said Sofi. "Maybe he really *was* here."

"Did he say anything to you in your dream?" asked Sal.

"He called me 'Little Gray Eyes' and told me not to worry about him," answered Sofi.

"Yeah, he talked to me, too," said Sal. "He told me he was going to go with Molly to the spirit world. I think that means he's going away."

"But I don't want him to go away!" said Sofi. She looked on the brink of tears.

"I don't either, but I'm afraid he will," said Sal. "Don't cry—we have to go downstairs in a minute!"

I called Sal a bit later and invited him and Sofi to go with us to look for the Christmas tree. The afternoon was cold, but the threat of snow was gone, so we stayed dry as we tromped through the trees at the Christmas tree farm. Ollie liked the really tall ones, but my dad reminded him that the biggest ones wouldn't fit inside our house. I tried to be excited about the Christmas tree, but couldn't stop feeling sad. Sal and I steered off to an area of fat spruce trees, away from the others, and he told me about the dreams he and Sofi had had the night before.

"I don't think they were dreams," I said. "I think Samuel came to your rooms."

"Yeah, I think so too. I'm worried about what he said. I'm pretty sure he was trying to tell us he's going away, to be with Molly."

Just then, Dad came through the trees and said, "I think we've found the right one! Come and take a look!"

The tree was perfect, so we had it cut and tethered to the top of the car. When we got it home, Dad set it upright in the garage. Mom said we could put it in the family room and decorate it later in the week. Sal asked us to come over for a while. We went to the basement while Sal told his parents that we would be working on school stuff until dinner. Just to be safe, he closed the basement door as he went down. We all went into the back room, which was dimly lit in the afternoon light.

No one said anything as Sal picked up the marble bag and rattled it. "Samuel! Samuel! Please come out!" he whispered.

"Your parents are upstairs!" said Ollie.

"I know, but we have to take the chance. After what Samuel said in my dream, I'm afraid we're not going to see him anymore!"

In a moment, Samuel appeared, still wearing Sal's hoodie, sweatshirt and jeans. I nearly fainted with relief. "I was afraid you weren't going to be here!" I said.

Samuel looked at us for a moment, then said, "You know that I found the spirit of my sister at the cemetery. It is time for me to go and join her in the spirit world."

Sofi threw her arms around him. "Please don't go! I love you!" she cried.

Samuel put his hands on her shoulders. "Did you hear me talking to you in the night?" he asked. "I tried to tell you not to worry, that I will be safe in the spirit world where I can be with my sister and parents. They have been waiting a long time for me."

"But we'll miss you!" said Ollie.

"And I will miss you," said Samuel. "But your world is not my world. I cannot stay here any longer, and now that I have found Molly, I can go and make our family complete again. You would do the same for your family, I know."

Sal, with a lump in his throat, said, "When will you go?"

"Soon," said Samuel. "But I wanted to tell you good-bye, and thank you for helping me. You have been the best friends that I could hope for. I wish I could repay you for what you did for me, but I know I cannot. So I will just say that I will be forever grateful."

Sofi was really crying by now, and Ollie's lip was quivering. I felt tears on my cheeks. Everyone stepped toward Samuel and we all hugged him tightly.

"Please do not be sad," said Samuel. "I think it is best for you to go now. And remember, I will always be your brother." As we stood in the huddle, Samuel silently disappeared for the last time.

"EVERYBODY STOP CRYING!" SAID Sal. "What will we say to Mom and Dad?" We all ran outside, hoping the cold air would somehow erase the grief from our faces. After a few minutes, Mrs. Martelli called Sal and Sofi for dinner, and Ollie and I slowly trudged home.

Chapter 27

Samuel's Gifts

Back at school on Monday, a new buzz was in the air, as everyone was already talking about Christmas and the winter holidays. Groups of kids shared tales of their Thanksgiving meals, visitors, and plans for Christmas.

I had a hard time getting through the day. "Why're you in such a bad mood?" asked Mady at lunchtime. "Didn't you have a great holiday?"

"Yeah, it was really good. We ate a lot, and we got our Christmas tree. I think I'm just tired out," I said.

Sal sat with a group of boys from his homeroom. They were talking excitedly about what they wanted for Christmas. Sal laughed with them, but didn't join in the chatter. When the lunch aide waved us out of the cafeteria to go to our homerooms, I passed Sal and whispered, "Meet me after school by our front walk."

Later, Ollie and I waited in the cold afternoon air for Sal and Sofi to arrive. When they got there, I asked, "Is it safe to go check on Samuel?"

"Yeah, my mom's working today, so I'm watching Sofi till she gets home," replied Sal.

We all ran to the Martellis' and went straight to the basement. Everything looked the same as it always did, but somehow it felt different. Sal picked up the marble bag and rattled it. "Samuel? Are you here?" he called.

We waited in silence, but Samuel did not appear. After a few minutes, we all looked at one another sadly. "I guess he's really gone," I said.

Sal sighed. He started to turn and leave the room, when Sofi cried, "Look!"

Everyone turned to see Sofi pointing at the shelves where Samuel had always appeared. On the bottom shelf, neatly folded, were Sal's jeans, socks, sweatshirt, and hoodie. And on top of them lay a beautiful wooden hawk beside the pocketknife Sal had given Samuel.

"Whoa!" We all fell to our knees in front of the shelf. We took turns holding the hawk, rubbing its smooth body, and admiring the expert carving of its head and feathers. As we passed it around, Ollie said, "What's this?" He grabbed another object from beside the pocketknife.

"It's the other block of wood!" I cried. Ollie held another wood carving, this one not as finished and

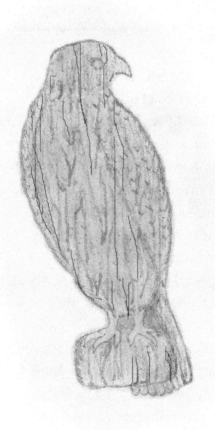

smooth as the hawk, but recognizable all the same. It was a carving of five people, heads and shoulders, lined up from tallest to shortest, with a girl on each end and three boys between them. The boy in the middle had what looked like a Mohawk haircut and a feather whittled into his chest.

"It's us—with Samuel!" cried Ollie.

"It's his gift to us," said Sal.

"Come on," I said. "We have to show Wally and Betty, and tell them Samuel is all right."

So, we all ran across the street and rang the Howards' doorbell. Wally invited us inside out of the cold, and we smelled fresh-baked bread from the kitchen.

"Just the four of you today?" asked Wally. "I thought you might have Samuel with you."

"Well, that's what we need to tell you about," I said. "Samuel's not homeless anymore. He's with his real family."

"Really? That's good news," said Wally, as Betty joined us from the kitchen. "Some relatives must have been located. Did they find him, or did he find them?"

"Uh, I think they found each other," said Sal.

"Do you think he's going to be OK?" asked Betty.

"We think so," I said. I nodded toward Sal. "Show them what he left for us."

Sal held out the carvings of the hawk and the children. Wally and Betty both admired Samuel's skill and workmanship. "Samuel was really grateful to you for helping him," Sal said. "He'd want you to know he's fine now."

"We were happy to help him," said Betty. "I wish we could have gotten to know him better, but I'm sure he's happy now that he has a home and family."

We all agreed, though it was hard to hide our sadness. "I can tell you're going to miss him," said Wally. "But put yourself in Samuel's place—what if you were lost and homeless, and then you found a family to live with? Wouldn't you be happy?"

"When we really love someone, we want what is best for them," said Betty. "I'm sure Samuel's family is thrilled to have him. Now why don't you all come in the kitchen for a slice of fresh bread?"

Chapter 28
Christmas Memories

I won't lie, it was really hard going back to life without Samuel. Most nights I laid in bed, thinking about all the good times we had and wondering where he was now. Where do ghosts go when they leave the real world? I guess I'll never really know, but I like to think Samuel is with his parents and sister somewhere.

I also thought a lot about what Samuel's life was like. It was so unfair! I tried to imagine what I would do if those things happened to me. It made me sad, and a little mad, to think about it. I'd never think about the Shawnee Indian Mission the same again.

Sal, Sofi, Ollie and I spent many afternoons talking about Samuel.

"What's your favorite memory of Samuel?" I asked the others. "I'll never forget the ride in Wally's car!"

"When we brought him upstairs!" said Sal.

"When he smiled at me and called me 'Little Gray Eyes,'" said Sofi.

"When he stood up to the bullies trying to steal our candy!" said Ollie.

All the fantastic memories cheered us up a little, but we still couldn't help feeling sad. Nobody said it, but I know none of us will *ever* forget that day in the cemetery.

"I wish he could have stayed here," said Ollie. Sofi nodded.

"Me, too," I said. "He could have been the big brother I wish I had."

"But that's why he had to go," said Sal. "I mean, one reason. Think about it—we'll all get older, and grow up and move away someday, but Samuel never would. He'd always be eleven years old. Even though I miss him, I know he couldn't stay with us."

"I never thought of it that way," I said. "And anyway, I know Betty was right—we really do want what's best for someone we love."

"I wish he could have stayed for Christmas," said Sofi.

"We didn't even talk to him about Christmas!" I said. "We never got to give him any presents!"

"But he gave some to us," said Ollie. "The wood carvings!"

"And he gave them to us because he loved us," said Sofi.

She's right, I thought. We give gifts (mostly) to people we love. Samuel didn't have much he could give us, just himself. Yeah, he gave us the wood carvings, but after all, *we* gave *him* the wood. But he truly was our friend. He never got angry or said mean things. He was smart, brave, kind and polite. I know he was grateful to us for helping him find Molly, but I think he would have done anything for us.

Yeah, he left, but not because he loved us less than we loved him. Like he said, our world isn't his world. Deep down, we knew he had to go. You've gotta do what you've gotta do.

WE DECIDED THAT SAL would keep the wooden hawk at their house. He set it on the lamp table beside his bed. He and Sofi would share it, and could always hold it whenever they were thinking of Samuel. Sal said when he thought of all the hours it had taken Samuel to make it, he felt lucky to have received such a fine gift.

We brought the carving of the five children to our house. I let Ollie keep it in his room in a special box where he kept his most treasured toys. I made him promise to let me see it whenever I wanted, and he solemnly agreed. "Just don't mess with any of my other stuff, OK?"

he said. I promised him I would not (because why would I want to?).

I put my drawing of Samuel in a box of special things I keep in my closet. It's not like I could ever forget what he looked like, but just in case. Maybe someday when I've had more practice, I can make it even better.

WINTER BREAK HAD BEGUN, and the Martellis were leaving the next day for the trip to New Jersey for Christmas. It was to be Sal's and Sofi's first airplane ride, and they could hardly wait. Sal had packed and repacked his clothes, and Sofi kept telling her mother more things she wanted to take with her.

"We can't take it all!" her mother said. "Besides, we'll be back in a week—you won't need everything you own!"

The four of us kids had agreed that for Christmas, we would exchange gifts with each other, but the gifts had to be something of our own that we wanted to pass on. Mr. and Mrs. Martelli came with Sal and Sofi to our house after dinner so we could give our gifts and say goodbye. My dad had a fire burning in the fireplace, and everyone gathered in the family room. The Christmas tree was all decorated and looked terrific. Mom brought in a tray of coffee and hot chocolate, and the grownups sat on the couch to watch us open our gifts.

Sal gave Ollie his superhero sheet set. He had decided that it was time to hand them down to someone who would appreciate them a while longer (he also whispered to Ollie that he had been sleeping on them when Samuel visited his room). Ollie was thrilled, and put the pillowcase on his head. Sal gave me a small bag of his marbles. They weren't antiques (he only had the one), but they were shiny and beautiful. I couldn't help thinking of Samuel when they clinked together. I promised to cherish them forever.

I gave Sofi a pair of pink- and purple-striped tights I had gotten for my one and only try at dance class in third grade. They looked as good as new, and I hoped they would remind her that Samuel thought of her as the dancing girl. Sofi loved them. I gave Sal the map of the Indian cemetery, which I had finished in colored pencil with some Wyandot symbols copied from the cemetery plaques. I could tell it meant a lot to him.

Ollie gave Sal his Kansas City Royals T-shirt, saying Sal needed to forget about the Mets. Sal thanked him, but said he would now have two favorite teams. Ollie gave Sofi a turtle beanbag he had had since he was about three. She already has a bazillion stuffed animals, but when she turned it over, she saw where he had drawn a feather on its belly with green marker.

Sofi gave Ollie her book about pirates, which had been handed down to her from Sal in the first place. Ollie whooped and ran over to show it to Mom and Dad. Sofi gave me the Princess Elsa necklace from her Halloween costume. She told me I was so pretty, I needed some nice jewelry, but I think she really wanted to remind me of that special Halloween.

Mrs. Martelli brought two jars of homemade spaghetti sauce, some special pasta shaped like bells and trees, and a huge plate of biscotti in different flavors—chocolate, cherry, and hazelnut. Mom and Dad gave the Martellis a jar of homemade jelly, a jar of Kansas City barbecue sauce, and a jigsaw puzzle with a picture of the Plaza lights.

Dad passed around the biscotti, then Mrs. Martelli said, "We've got a long day of travel tomorrow—time for everyone to head home for bed!" Sal and Sofi helped me and Ollie clean up all the wrapping paper and ribbons, then got ready to leave.

Everyone wished everyone else a Merry Christmas.

"We'll be back in time for New Year's," said Mrs. Martelli. "See you then!"

"Merry Christmas!" I said. "Have a safe trip!"

"And Merry Christmas to you," said Sal as he waved at the door. "I hope next year will be as exciting as this year was!"

Afterword

Places and Terms

The Shawnee Indian Mission was founded by Reverend Thomas Johnson, a Methodist minister, in what became present-day Johnson County, Kansas. Native American families sent their children to school there from 1839 until 1862. They lived in dormitories and studied English and vocational subjects such as home economics, farming and carpentry. After the Civil War, the government set up schools that forcibly took Native American children from their families in an effort to eradicate their culture and languages.

The Wyandot Nation was first encountered by European trappers in Ontario, Canada in the seventeenth century. The name 'Huron' was given to the Wendat, or Wyandot, by the French. They migrated west to Ohio after a war with other Native American nations. Following the terms of a treaty with the United States, they left Ohio and moved to Kansas in 1843. Like most other Native American nations, they were systematically and methodically forced westward as white settlers demanded their land for farming. Today the Wyandots live in Oklahoma, Kansas, Michigan and Canada.

Huron Indian Cemetery is officially named the Wyandot National Burying Ground. It is located in Kansas

City, Kansas, which is in Wyandotte County. It is estimated that between 400 and 600 individuals are buried there, most of whom are unnamed. There is indeed a gravestone for Ron-Ton-Dee, a Wyandot chief, who also had the name Warpole.

The Konza Prairie is a native tallgrass prairie preserve located in the Flint Hills in east-central Kansas. It is used for ecological research, education, and outreach.

Native American Moons do not actually correspond to our calendar months. Native American tribes had various names for the full moons, which they named to keep track of the seasons. There are thirteen full moons in most calendar years. Full moons don't fall on a particular day or even in a particular month. For example, sometimes the Harvest Moon falls in September, and sometimes in October.

Gunnysacks were large bags made of burlap fabric that were used to store hard fruits and vegetabes, nuts, or animal feed.

Black walnut trees are an American hardwood that grow all around eastern Kansas and western Missouri. The ripening walnuts have a distinct and recognizable scent.

The Country Club Plaza is a well-known outdoor shopping district in Kansas City, Missouri. Every year since 1930 the European-style buildings have been decorated with Christmas lights, which now number

280,000 bulbs. On Thanksgiving night, thousands of people gather there to watch as the lights are switched on for the Christmas season (usually by a celebrity).

Biscotti are twice-baked cookies that originated in Italy.

Kansas City is known for its world-famous barbecue.

References and Sources

David McLimans, *Big Turtle*, Walker Publishing Company, 2011

The Trail of Tears of the Wyandot Indians by Paul Edelman and Jill Draper, Martin City Telegraph, November 23, 2018

William E. Connelly, *A Standard History of Kansas and Kansans, vol. 1, The Wyandots*, Chicago: Lewis Publishing Co., 1918. Reprinted at Wyandotte-nation. org

The Wyandot Nation of Kansas website

Native-languages.org, Wyandot Indian Culture and History, Laura Redish and Orrin Lewis, 1998

Legendsofamerica.com, Wyandot-Huron Tribe, copyright Kathy Weiser/Legends of Kansas, updated October 2018

Joseph Bruchac, *Children of the Longhouse*, Dial Books for Young Readers, New York, 1996

Joseph Bruchac, *Code Talker: A Novel About the Navajo Marines of World War Two*, Dial Books, New York, 2005

About the Author

A lifelong Kansan, Fran Borin grew up hearing about the turbulent, sometimes violent history of the eastern part of the state. Bleeding Kansas, the Border War, stops on the Underground Railroad—all were within a few miles of her childhood home, and didn't seem that long ago to her. In spite of a deep and abiding interest in history, Fran's working life consisted of teaching, motherhood, and federal law enforcement. One day she read a newspaper article that reported ghost sightings near the Shawnee Indian Mission. She mulled it over for the next twenty-five years, and the result was the story of Samuel Grayhawk.

Fran lives with her husband within walking distance of the Shawnee Indian Mission. She has three grown children.